Act Well Your Part

Don Sakers

ACT WELL YOUR PART
copyright © 1986, Don Sakers

Published by
Speed-of-C Productions
811 Camp Meade Rd
Linthicum, MD 21090

ISBN: 978-1934754-221
February 2020

Dedication:

*To my fellow 1976 members of Thespian Troupe 2347:
Ann, Bonnie, both Debbies, Doreen, Helen, Jill, Karen,
Kathy, Linda, Mark, Mike, Ray, Rick, Steve, and Tom.*

Author's Note:

Act Well Your Part does not take place in our world. Oak Grove High School exists only in that misty, far-off place called "The Best of All Possible Worlds." It is a parallel universe just a few steps away, a world in which sexual orientation matters only as much as eye color or left-handedness, and young love is a sweet and beautiful thing for all young lovers.

This is an unabashed romance story, set a few decades ago, not in the world as it was, but in the world as, perhaps, it *should have been.*

Act Well Your Part is a piece of fiction. But I know that my readers join with me in the fervent hope that one day we may live in a world in which high school students, teachers, parents, and the general public will be just as accepting as the characters in this book.

Don Sakers

CHAPTER ONE

Keith Graff looked at his watch and stifled a moan. Only two-thirty. It seemed that this class would never end.

Miss Spivak continued her lecture, and Keith stared out the window. It wasn't that he didn't like the class...but tryouts for the fall play were this afternoon after school, and this was the last period of the day.

Outside it was a glorious October day. The sky was abroil with fast-moving clouds in every shade of grey and white, and a crisp wind darted through the schoolground, carrying odd bits of trash as it went. Keith knew that it was chilly outside, a delicious kind of chilly that would have found him sitting by the fire to do his homework, back in the other house. Here, of course, they had no fireplace.

Old windowpanes rattled in their frames, and Keith could hardly contain his restlessness. This was a time of year for possibilities, when the smell of burning leaves filled the air and energies that had run free all summer could be chained and disciplined to new tasks.

Miss Spivak droned on, and Keith snuck another look at his watch. Twenty-five minutes to go!

Until last week Keith had wanted time to stand still, or preferably to move backwards. It had been a busy summer, what with Mom getting a new job and the two of them moving to Oak Grove just in time for Keith to start the school year in a new school. And he'd hated it.

He had been all set to spend his last two years at dear old familiar Kinwood Senior High. Finishing sophomore year near the top of his class, he had a comfortable circle of friends and was anticipating a marvelous year in eleventh grade.

Well, that was all over now. And he'd hated Oak Grove. Hated the idea of being without friends, hated being the new kid who didn't fit in anywhere, even hated the dingy twenty-year-old brick building itself.

Then tryouts were announced, and Keith decided the new school wasn't so bad after all. He had always enjoyed acting, and was involved in dramatics at Kinwood. Here was a chance to get involved in something he liked, to get to know some of his classmates, and finally to have a way to fit in. Keith didn't mind if he got just a minor part—all he wanted was to be involved in the play.

If this stupid class would ever end!

When the bell eventually rang Keith was up out of his seat in a flash. He threw his books into his knapsack and raced out the door,. threaded his way through the crowded halls, just about flew down the main stairs, and skidded to a halt in the broad corridor outside the auditorium. Sure enough, there was the sign: "TRYOUTS FOR FALL PLAY here after school."

The door was locked; Keith waited as patiently as he could until the drama teacher, Mr. Hening ("Call me Bob") showed up. Hening grinned when he saw Keith leaning against the auditorium door.

"Hello, Keith. I knew you were eager, but I didn't think you were going to be the first one here." From a belt hook Hening produced a jumble of keys and fumbled through them trying to unlock the door. "You could have stopped for a coke. It'll take me a while to set up."

"Is there anything I can do to help?"

"Not unless you know which key unlocks this door. Ah, *here* it is." He inserted the key, tried to turn it, and swore under his breath. "No, that's not it either."

"Third from the end," a new voice said.

"Thank you, Bran." Hening unlocked the door, then put an arm on Keith's shoulder and turned him to meet the newcomer. "This is Keith Graff, from my second-period class.

He's destined to be the next Peter O'Toole, so watch out for him. Keith, meet Bran Davenport."

Bran Davenport was two or three inches taller than Keith—five-foot-ten or -eleven. His short black hair was a little mussed. He wore a threadbare t-shirt imprinted on the front with "Oak Grove Stage Crew." Bran's dark eyebrows gave him a somewhat satanic look, but his boyish face and easy smile softened the impact. A slight growth of downy fuzz lined his chin.

"Please to meet you, Keith." Bran carried a cardboard box filled with playbooks; he balanced it on one leg and offered his right hand to Keith.

Bran's grip was warm and firm; his hands were slightly bigger than Keith's but his fingers were thinner. His fingernails were trimmed; Keith, an incurable nail-biter, felt a little ashamed of his own hands.

Hening patted Keith on the back, then held open the door. "Let's get inside now, that box can't be light." As Bran passed him, Hening looked back at Keith and said in a stage-whisper, "When Bran signed up to be a last-period drama aide, he didn't know I'd be using him as a beast of burden."

From the darkness ahead Bran laughed. "Don't let him kid you, Keith. Bob uses *everyone* as a beast of burden."

"You can transfer to social studies if you want," Hening offered, jokingly.

"What, and leave show business?"

The auditorium was lit only by two glowing green EXIT signs over the doors; Keith moved carefully to avoid bumping into something. He was impressed by the way Bran and Bob Hening moved with calm assurance. Bran put his box down on the stage, leaped up, and vanished into the wings. A few seconds later there was a massive "thump" and the house lights came up.

"Why don't you take a seat, Keith; everyone else will be here soon." Hening jumped onto the stage himself, and went into the back with Bran.

A few more kids trickled in while Mr. hening and Bran adjusted the spotlights, and finally Hening appeared onstage to give a little pep talk about the fall play, and how he knew that everyone wanted a part but after all there were only a limited number and he hoped everyone would help out even if they didn't get a role in the play. It was the same speech that the drama teacher at Kinwood used to give, and Keith idly wondered if all drama teachers knew it.

Keith was one of the first people to go on. He gave a short speech from *Man of LaMancha*, the speech that his friend Frank had delivered last year during Kinwood's production. Keith had worked with Frank so often on the bit, he knew it inside and out.

"Thank you," Hening said. "We'll post the cast list on the drama room door by tomorrow morning. You can stick around if you'd like."

As he walked down the stairs off the stage, Keith saw Bran Davenport flash him a smile and make a thumbs-up motion. At least *someone* thought he had done well.

Keith had told his mother he would call her for a ride home, and she wouldn't be back from work until at least five-thirty. It was only about three-thirty now; he decided to hang around for a while and see how everyone else did. One or two of the other kids were good, better than he was…and quite a few were worse. Even some that he knew were leading lights in the Drama Club.

When Bran Davenport came on stage, Keith sat up in his wooden seat and brushed back his hair. This year's play was *Arsenic and Old Lace*; Bran delivered from memory a speech from the second act, with one of the senior girls reading all the other parts.

When he finished, Bran came into the auditorium and sat down next to Keith. "Hey, you did pretty well."

"So did you. A lot better than I did."

"Well, I've probably had a lot more experience than you. Hening is a good director. You're new at Oak Grove, aren't you?"

"This is my first year. I'll say you've had experience. Didn't you play the lead in the spring musical last year?"

"A fan. How did you know that?"

"Mr. Hening showed us old programs in drama class. I recognized your name."

At that minute Mr. hening looked right at Bran and frowned. "Bran, perhaps you could extend your fellow actors the courtesy of being quiet through their tryouts? Thank you."

Bran smiled and motioned to Keith. "Come on, let's go out in the hall. Then we can talk."

"Okay."

After school a coke machine was set up in the hallway between the cafeteria and the auditorium; the two boys bought soft drinks and then sat against the brick wall. Bran held up his can. "To a successful audition."

"Cheers." Both took a sip, and then Keith sighed. "What part are you after?"

"Teddy."

"I thought you'd go for the lead."

"Nah. Jerry Todd is going to get Mortimer. It's a simple part, and Jerry needs the experience. I'm hoping Bob will let me tackle Teddy. What a *great* part." For a second he fell into a Teddy Roosevelt impersonation. "Bully, bully!" He took another sip of coke. "Did your old school have a chapter of the Thespian Society?"

Keith nodded. He was well acquainted with the international society of high school dramatists. "Yeah. I had two and a half points when I left Kinwood." Points were awarded for various activities connected with dramatics, from prop-management and costumes to directing and playing the starring roles in a performance. Ten points were enough to become a Thespian.

"Well hell, we'll have you initiated by the end of the year, then. You can carry over points from your last school, you know." A last swig of coke, and Bran crushed the can absently.

"I'd like that."

There seemed no way to continue the conversation, and yet Keith didn't want Bran to leave. He looked sideways at the older boy, and for a second Bran met his eyes. They stared at one another for a few second, then Keith turned his head away, a little embarrassed. "I guess I'd better be getting home."

"How are you getting there?"

Keith shrugged. "Walk, I guess. My mom won't be home for a while yet."

Bran stood up, a process that he accomplished with a throw of his shoulders and levitation. "Want a ride home? I've got a car, and I'll be giving a couple of the others a lift. You can't be too far out of the way."

Keith stood, trying to conceal a sudden shiver. "If it's not putting you out too much."

"Okay, then. Debbie and Laura ought to be done by now. Let me get them, and we can go." Bran dashed into the auditorium, and Keith leaned back against the wall. His knees felt weak.

Whoa, Keith boy, he thought to himself. Take it easy. You've just met the guy. Star actor, and good-looking to boot... he probably has half the girls in the senior class crawling over him. He's probably going steady with one of them. He's probably....

Bran was back, with two girls. "Keith Graff, this is Debbie Vovcenko and Laura Birtonelli. Keith is new here."

Debbie, a thin redhead, waved her fingers. "Pleased to meet you. How do you like Oak Grove?"

"Okay, I guess. I'm still getting used to it, I mean."

Laura, a short, chubby dark-haired girl, smiled. "Just don't let anyone try to sell you an elevator pass or send you to the pool with a message." She shrugged. "No elevator, no pool. They caught me with both of them when I was a freshman."

"Thanks for the warning."

Bran put his arms around Debbie's shoulder, and Keith did his best not to react. "We're going to drop Keith at home, if you girls don't mind."

Laura chuckled. "Keith, *you* must be the one who minds. If you've never seen Bran drive...."

"I haven't."

"Well, you're in for quite an experience."

Bran started toward the door with Debbie, then looked over his shoulder. "Nobody's died yet."

"No fault of your."

"You can always walk if you want."

Laura snatched at Keith's hand. "Come on, he's just liable to leave without us."

It was only a fifteen-minute drive from school to Keith's house. He couldn't find anything to fault about Bran's driving; in his opinion the older boy drove with great care. Keith had been in cars where all he could do was hold onto the seat and pray he would survive—Bran drove better than his mother.

When Bran pulled up in front of the two-story frame house that Keith was only now beginning to call home, Keith opened the car door and put one foot on the ground. "Thanks for the ride. Hey, can I ask you guys in for a drink or something?"

"Thanks for the offer, kid. But I have to get Debbie home, she's got to be at work in half an hour."

"Oh. Okay." Keith tried not to show his disappointment, and he didn't think he succeeded completely.

"But now that I know where you live, I mean, well, you'll probably be staying after school for rehearsals, I could give you a ride sometimes."

"Hey, I wouldn't want you to have to go out of your way."

"We can talk about it later. Don't forget that the cast list will be posted tomorrow."

"I'll be there bright and early." Keith waved. "Nice to meet you, Debbie, Laura. And thanks again," he said to Bran.

The older boy gave him a smile, and the car pulled away.

Keith let himself into the house, threw his books on his bed, and went to the kitchen to fix himself a snack. He glanced at the morning paper still scattered about the kitchen table, and read half the front page without paying attention while he nibbled cookies.

Something was happening. Again.

It had been like this with Frank—except, with Frank, it had come on slowly. Frank and Keith had been friends since elementary school, and only during the last year had Keith come to realize that he cared about Frank more than one friend usually cared about another.

They had skirted the issue, enough for Keith to be sure that Frank felt the same way…and then Mom got her new job, and Keith moved. And just as well, he thought at the time, because it was after all a pretty scary thing. And for all that he missed Frank, he was also glad that nothing had… happened.

He crumpled his paper towel, ricocheted it off the refrigerator into the trash can, and rinsed his glass in the sink. Be honest, fella, he said to himself as he looked out the window at the cloudy October sky. Bran Davenport probably doesn't even like boys, at least not in the way *you're* thinking of. And if he did, which was a pretty big if, even if he *did* he probably wouldn't give you a second look. He's a senior, member of the Thespians, star of last year's play, and aide to the drama teacher. You're a newcomer, lower than a freshman.

Forget it, Keith. Your job is to get yourself accepted by some of the other kids at school. You did a good job today with Bran and the two girls, just keep it up. And don't cause trouble by letting your feelings lead you into doing something stupid.

Keith turned on the television, and an hour and a half later his mother found him there when she walked in the door. "Okay, son, get up. You set the table and I'll get dinner. Then there's time for you to gather up the trash before we eat."

"Aw, Mom...."

She tousled his hair. "Don't 'Aw, Mom' me, trash day is tomorrow and you know you're not going to feel like it later tonight." She kissed him. "How did school go?"

"Okay."

"Didn't you have play tryouts today?" She looked at her watch as they moved to the kitchen. "I thought I'd have to come get you."

"I got a ride with some kids who tried out."

"That's good." She started making dinner while Keith cleared away the paper and set the table. As he worked he told his mother about the fall play, about Mr. hening, about his history class and the latest experiment in physics, and about the TV shows he's watched while waiting for her to come home.

After the table was set Keith went about the house emptying trash cans, and dragged the big metal can out to the curb for the garbage men. Rain or shine, they would be here at six o'clock tomorrow morning, their truck snorting and can lids crashing, and Keith would know it was time to get up. He never overslept on Tuesdays and Fridays.

On the way back to the house Keith looked up at the sky. About half of it was obscured by clouds...but there was a gibbous moon dating in and out of the clouds, and where the sky was clear the stars shone through with bright jewel-like light. For a while he stood in his shirtsleeves, looking at the sky and smelling the clean air. Then he caught himself shivering and went back inside.

During dinner his mother read the latest letter from his grandmother, and they spent the rest of the meal in animated conversation about various relatives.

Over dessert Keith's mother stared at him and a smile played around the corners of her mouth. "Offhand, I'd say you like Oak Grove a lot more than you did a week ago."

"What makes you say that?"

"You've been talking nonstop since I walked in the door. A week ago all you said was variations on 'I hate Oak Grove and I wish we had never moved.'"

Keith laughed. "Yeah, I guess I *was* in a bad mood."

"So why the change?"

"I don't know. Tryouts, I guess."

"You're probably right." She stood, picked up her plate and Keith's, and started loading the dishwasher. Chuckling, she said, "One thing's for sure, this is a different Keith than the one who lived here last week. And I think I like the improvement." She was silent for a moment. "An outside observer would probably decide that you were in love."

"Mother."

"I know, I know, it's none of my business."

"I'm *not* in love. I'm just in a better mood because of tryouts."

"Oh, I know. I was just telling you what an outside observer would say."

Trying to hide a blush, Keith handed her the dirty glasses and then turned away. "I'm going to my room. I have some homework to do."

She smiled tenderly. "Don't forget that movie you want to see is on at nine tonight."

"I won't forget." Keith went to his room, took out his history book, and did his best to lose himself in studying.

CHAPTER TWO

Morning had never been Keith's favorite time of day. When his clock radio went off he rolled over and glared at the digital display, hoping against hope that his gaze would intimidate the thing and it would shut. It didn't work. Instead, the garbage truck turned onto the street with its customary racket.

Keith took a quick shower and stood in the middle of his room, wondering what to wear. His favorite jeans, of course— but what shirt? He finally settled on a green pullover that his father had sent out for his birthday. The shirt was attractive and Keith didn't mind that it was a little tight.

"Son, you're running late."

"Okay, Mom." Keith pulled on socks and bounded down the stairs into the kitchen, his hair still damp. He poured a bowl of cereal and a cup of coffee. Usually as much milk went into his coffee as went on his cereal, but today he stopped with a bare trickle and left the coffee quite dark. "I've decided to start drinking it with less milk," he announced.

His mother nodded over her own mug. "I knew it would come sooner of later. My little boy is growing up." Her smile told him that she was kidding.

"Mom, don't think of it as me growing up. Think of it as *you* getting older."

"Touché." She sipped, then looked at the clock with alarm. "Hurry up, eat. We're going to be late."

Keith obediently downed the rest of his cereal, blew on his coffee and managed to get most of it down. At the look on his face, Mrs. Graff laughed. "Tastes better with milk, doesn't it? Don't worry, you'll soon develop a tolerance." She stood, took her briefcase from the coat rack and handed Keith his windbreaker. "It's supposed to be breezy today."

"Thanks." Keith rinsed his cup and bowl quickly, slid his feet into his sneakers, and snatched up his schoolbooks. "You're sure you don't mind running me by school?"

"Not at all. It's right on my way." They left the house and got into the car. As she slid into the driver's seat, Keith's mother asked, "What's on the agenda for today? Will you be riding the bus home?"

"Probably. But if I got a part, Mr. Hening might want to have practice or something after school. If so I'll manage to get home somehow."

The car roared to life. "No hitchhiking. You understand me?"

"Yes, Mother. If I stay, I might have a friend drive me home." The thought of getting another ride from Bran Davenport made Keith feel inwardly warm despite the autumn chill.

"Whatever. If you're not at home when I get back from work I'll send the Army our looking for you."

"Right."

In front of the school, his mother pulled over to the curb and leaned across the car to give Keith a quick kiss. "Have a good day. I hope you got a part."

"It doesn't matter. If I didn't I'll still get involved."

"That's the spirit."

It was still early—almost a full hour before school started, at least half an hour before the buses arrived. Keith had never seen school this early; he walked around the neatly-kept grass toward the shop wing and marveled at the stillness. Most of the teachers were here, undoubtedly…but he had the grounds almost to himself as far as students were concerned.

One of the large industrial arts classrooms in a brick annex building had been set aside as the drama room. There Mr.

Hening had set up a small stage complete with serviceable floodlights. Keith liked the drama room; it had its own personality.

The door was locked, but the lights were on and Mr. Hening's car was parked right outside the building. Maybe, Keith thought, Hening was in the faculty lounge having a last cup of coffee before the day started. Oh, well, he wasn't interested in seeing Mr. Hening. His attention was captured by a neatly-typed piece of paper held to the door by two pieces of faded masking tape.

The cast list.

Keith ran his eyes down the list quickly as he held his breath. He felt disappointment, but then...yes...there was his name. MR. WITHERSPOON: Keith Graff.

Breathing a great sigh, Keith slumped against the cold brick wall and pounded his hands against it in barely-suppressed joy. I got a part. I got a part.

He took another breath and looked again, Yes, there it was: TEDDY BREWSTER: Bran Davenport. So Bran got the part he wanted. That was good.

There was a crunch of car tires on gravel behind him, and Keith turned to see the already-familiar red Plymouth, Bran's car. Bran killed the motor and hopped out, accompanied by a short, somewhat dumpy fellow. Bran wore jeans and a black windbreaker zipped all the way up.

"Morning, Keith," Bran said, then pushed past Keith to look at the cast list. He let out a whoop of excitement. "I made it."

"Congratulations," Keith said, offering his hand. Bran took it, pumped Keith's arm vigorously, and slapped him on the back. Then he stopped suddenly, looked at the list again. "Oh, thank god, you made it too. It would have been very tacky to celebrate if you'd lost out."

Bran's friend was standing next to the car with his arms folded across his chest. "If you don't mind...."

"Oh, right. First things first. Keith, this is Albert Travis, known to all his friends as Bert. Bert, Keith Graff...our newest victim."

Shaking hands with Albert was like picking up a half pound of raw ground beef while making hamburgers. "Victim?" Keith echoed.

Albert nodded slowly. "Bran means that you're the newest person to join our little clique." He looked at Bran, tossed his head. "I don't suppose you'd be willing to tell me if *I'm* involved in this show?"

Bran put himself in front of the list, crossed his arms. "Why do you have to look? You *know* you got it."

Albert fixed Bran with a steady gaze. "I am being patient with you." his tone told Keith that Albert was not all that amused by bran's sense of humor...but that he had resigned himself to it long ago.

"Here, look." Bran spun, ran his finger down the list. "There. Stage Manager: Albert Travis." He winked at Keith. "Actors are a dime a dozen, but a good stage manager is worth his weight in M&Ms." He turned back to the list. "Debbie got Abby. And Laura is playing Officer O'Hara." He seemed to contemplate the choices, nodded. "Laura isn't going to get anywhere as long as she stays so tense."

"Well," Albert said, "At least she's better than *I* am."

"Careful, Bert, or I'll agree with you." Bran clapped his arms around himself to give a quick impersonation of a man freezing to death on Mount Everest. "I am *cold*. Let's get inside."

Albert followed Bran, and Keith tagged along, not sure if the invitation had included him. As they entered the main building, Bran held the door and stuck his palm out for a tip; Albert ignored him and Keith dug in his pocket for a coin, dropped it in Bran's palm.

"Thank you, kind sir," Bran said, going down on one knee and holding out an arm in a dramatic pose. Keith held back a giggle and did his best to nod in a dignified fashion. His best was none too good.

Still kneeling, Bran reached up to touch the tail of Keith's shirt. "A fine piece of apparel, my good man," he said in Shakespearean style. "You must give me the name of your tailor." Then Bran was up on his feet, overflowing with energy.

Before classes started the students had the run of the school building; Keith followed Bran and Albert down the main corridor without really knowing where they were headed. Along the way, Bran kept up a running conversation. "Are you satisfied with your part?"

"Sure," Keith said at once. Then he chuckled. "Although I'm not really sure what part Mr. Witherspoon *is*," he admitted.

"Comes in at the very end. Head of the sanitarium or something like that. It's a good part, I think you'll have a lot of fun with it."

"I'll say."

In front of the library, Bran was assaulted by the flying body of Debbie Vovcenko. She threw her arms around him and gave him a theatrical kiss. "Did you see? Did you see?"

"Yes. Bert got Stage Manager."

"*I* got Abby. Pity you didn't get Mortimer."

"Jerry got Mortimer. I *told* you he would. But who listens to me?"

Debbie tugged Bran's arm. "Come on, Laura has pictures from the picnic. You ought to see how stupid Warren looks."

Bran looked back at Keith, gave him a tiny wave. "Catch you later. Okay?"

"Sure." Then Bran and Albert were gone, dragged into the library by Debbie. Keith sighed, then started walking toward his first-period classroom. For a moment he felt sad, then he hugged his books to himself and smiled.

He'd gotten a part!

He hardly noticed the rest of the day.

*

The first rehearsal was not until a week after tryouts. Mr. Hening said the delay was to give those students with jobs a chance to work out their schedules. "But I want to see all cast members in the auditorium Monday after school," he said, "and no excuses."

Several times during the next week Keith ran into Bran and his friends in the halls, and each time Bran waved to him and made some witty comment, or introduced yet another of his vast number of acquaintances. Keith learned that Bran took Play Production in the drama room immediately after his own Acting Arts class second period, and took to hanging around the room until the older boy arrived, just so he could trade "good mornings."

He wished, just a little, that Bran would have more to do with him…but at the same time he was glad that the older boy was not becoming too close a friend too quickly.

At lunch Keith saw Bran and his friends at a table across the cafeteria. Bran's table was always noisy…Bran's other friends seemed to be as high-spirited as Bran, with the exception of the quiet Albert. For the first two days Keith walked by the table several times, hoping to be noticed. Then he went back to sitting at his own table in the corner, and ate in silence.

They probably don't want the newcomer sitting with them, Keith thought to himself. Everybody is waiting to see where I'll fit in before they start having anything to do with me. Well, i don't do drugs, and I can't play football so I'll never be a jock, and I'm not in the Student Government. Sooner or later I'll find a niche with these drama people.

I hope.

Finally it was Monday, and Keith once again sat through endless classes waiting for bells that seemed as if they must be out of order. He came to lunch convinced that the day was actually over, and that the entire school had fallen into a time warp. It would *never* be time for play practice.

His sandwich had no taste; he ate it automatically and then fished in his lunch bag to see what else Mom had packed.

"Ahem."

He looked up to see Laura Birtonelli. Her eye twinkled. "All right, Keith Graff, it is time to stop being a man of mystery."

"Huh?"

"Huh?" she repeated. "What command of the language." Her smile told him that she was kidding. "I have been sent as an official delegation to ask your presence at our humble table. Everyone in the cast is wondering what you're like, and Bran is no help at all."

"I...."

"Tell us when you get there." She picked up his books, and Keith meekly followed her to Bran's table.

"Well, well," Debbie said. "The loner finally shows his face. Sit down, we don't bite."

Six pairs of eyes were on him, and Keith fought not to blush. Bran was at one end of the table and Albert at the other; Keith sat down next to Bran. Laura put his books down in front of him, then struck a pose and cleared her throat. "Ladies, Gentlemen, and Debbie: May I present Keith Graff, who will entertain the school as Mr. Witherspoon in his first appearance on the Oak Grove stage. Keith, you know Bran, and you've met Debbie and me. That is Bert, and this is Jane Larson, and over there is Warren Briggs. Say hello to the nice man, folks."

Bran clapped Keith on the back. "Sorry I didn't think to invite you over sooner. It was Laura's idea. You looked so forlorn sitting over there all alone."

"Thanks, all of you." Jane Larson was a pretty girl with red hair; Keith knew from the cast list that she would play the other major female role besides Debbie's. Warren Briggs was tall, thin, and dark, and he sat back in his chair like a king surveying his court. He played one of the numerous police officers.

Feeling nervous, Keith dug in his lunch bag and produced an apple. He started to crunch noisily at it, and tried to fit into the conversation that seethed around him. It was difficult to do, since he knew none of the people being discussed.

At last the bell rang, and everyone gathered up their books. Bran smiled to Keith. "See you after school. Get there as soon as you can, Bob doesn't like having to wait for people."

"I will."

The second bell rang, and everyone dispersed. Keith moved as quickly as he could to his next class, American History, and daydreamed through the lecture.

When school was over he was the first one in front of the auditorium door. M<r. Hening and Bran arrived together, and Hening handed Keith a blue playbook. "Welcome aboard, Keith. I think you'll do a fine job. And we're glad to have you as part of the troupe." He frowned. "Bran, which one of these damned keys *is* it?"

"Third from the end," both Bran and Keith said in unison. They both burst out laughing.

The meeting was really just an organizational session; Hening introduced each of the cast members and explained the rehearsal schedule. "I'm not going to ask that you be here when you're not rehearsing your scenes, but it wouldn't be a bad idea to stick around whenever you can and watch the others at work. Remember, we're a *cast* and not a bunch of individuals who just stumbled in and decided to do a play. Bert, do you have anything to add?"

Albert stood up in his seat, a ludicrous figure. "Just all the usual stuff. Don't be late, make sure you put your props back where they belong, and remember to tip the stage manager for all services." There was polite laughter.

Hening clapped. "All right, people. The meeting is over. Names and phone numbers on the list on the piano, and then take some time to look around the stage and facilities. You should know this stage well, it's your second home."

Keith lined up with the others to give his name and phone number, then hopped up on stage and wandered behind the curtains. The ropes, lights, and curtains looked similar to those at Kinwood. He felt sure he could easily get used to this stage.

Backstage there were two prop rooms, and two ladders that led up to caged areas. Keith was staring up one of them when Bran bounced up behind him.

"That's no way to see. Come on, let's go up."

"What's up there?"

"Lighting deck. Go on up."

The iron ladder felt firm under Keith's hands; he climbed swiftly and stepped onto the concrete surface of the lighting deck. The controls themselves, a huge grey metal bulk with numerous large levers and switches, overlooked the stage so that the stage crew could have a good view of everything that went on below them.

"Nice," Keith said, running his hands over the controls but careful to change nothing. "This looks pretty new."

"We had the board replaced two years ago. The old one was condemned as a fire hazard." Bran took the two largest levers firmly in his hands, looking like a pirate captain at the wheel of his ship. "Watch."

He pulled the levers and spotlights came up on the stage. More levers, and the stage lights brightened red, blue, yellow, and green.

"Davenport, leave those lights alone!" Mr. Hening shouted from the stage, without even looking in Bran's direction.

"Yessir," Bran snapped, saluting as he said it. He turned back to Keith with a grin. "Come on back this way."

"What's back here?" They moved past a rack containing spotlight housings, bulbs, and a tangle of black and red wires. The space narrowed, and then there was another ladder set in a wall of cinderblocks.

"This goes up to the catwalk." Bran paused with his hand on the ladder. "You're not afraid of heights, are you?"

"Not really."

"Good. You'll like it up here." Bran climbed the ladder, and Keith followed him.

The catwalk ran up close to the roof of the auditorium, a latticework of strong black iron that hung above the ceiling of acoustical tile. It ran across the entire front of the auditorium, and Keith saw massive spotlights suspended next to the catwalk, aimed at the stage.

Bran moved forward, stooping, and held onto a handrail that looked none too substantial. Keith followed him.

It was rather nice up here—secluded, and kind of peaceful. Bran stopped next to one of the huge spots, letting his hand rest on the massive piece of equipment. Keith stood next to him.

"Look," Bran said, and Keith leaned forward. He saw the stage far below, and the kids who stood upon it. And suddenly it all seemed very real to him. "Wow," he said, trying to find some way to express his feeling. "This is like a real play. I mean, not high school at all. Looking down from here, I can imagine that this is a real stage with real actors, on Broadway or something."

"It *is* real, Keith. There's no difference between us and real actors. Except they have more experience. And they get paid."

"Are you going to be an actor?"

Bran looked sideways at Keith. "I *am* an actor."

"I mean…when you finish school. Do you want to act for a living?"

"I've considered it," bran said, noncommittally.

Keith looked down at the stage. "Wouldn't be a bad thing to do with your life."

Keith's hands were firmly gripping the handrail. Bran moved his right hand from the spotlight, put it down almost casually next to Keith's. He looked straight ahead and Keith tried to keep his eyes on the stage…but he was conscious of

Bran's hand next to his, and he felt as if an electrical current from one of the big black cables were running through him, sharpening his senses and making him glow with possibilities.

Calm down, Keith boy, he told himself. I'm sure he's not....

"Hey, what are you two doing up here?" Jerry Todd, the clean-cut senior who was playing the male lead, poked his head up onto the catwalk. Bran jerked his hand back as if stung by a bee, then took a step away from Keith.

"What do you *think* we're doing?" Bran said. "We're looking at the stage."

Jerry shrugged. "Well, I don't know, maybe you guys are...you know." His tone of casual cruelty was completely unintentional, Keith knew, but just the same he was glad it was dark and Bran couldn't see him blush.

Bran laughed. "Sure we are. Do you want to join us?" Keith gripped the rail even harder, his knuckles turning white —but Bran was just joking.

"Well," Jerry said, "Bob wants you guys to come down. He's going to close up the auditorium. And remember to turn off the lights when you come."

"Okay." Bran waved Keith before him, and they descended to the stage without a word.

Once again Bran drove Keith home, accompanied not only by Debbie and Laura but also Albert. On the ride Bran was his usual bubbly self, and Keith all but forgot the incident on the catwalk.

After dinner he excuse himself to do more studying. His mother cocked her head and looked concerned. "You haven't been very talkative. Are you feeling all right?"

"I'm okay. I'm just a little tired from all the excitement today. I think I'll go to bed early tonight."

She let him go without any further comment, for which Keith was grateful. He spent two hours reading history and English and doing algebra, then undressed and crawled into bed.

It was a chilly night, just perfect for snuggling up under the covers and going to sleep, but still it was well past midnight when Keith finally drifted into a restless sleep.

CHAPTER THREE

Rehearsal brought a new kind of order to Keith's life. Each day he stayed after school until five or six o'clock, then Bran dropped him off at home by six-fifteen at the latest. His mother held dinner, and after his meal he spent a few hours on his homework. Exhausted, he was in bed by ten each night.

And slowly, as the weather became chillier, Keith's days started glowing with an inner warmth like logs brightly ablaze in a cozy fireplace.

Rehearsal was always the high point of his day. Since his character didn't come in until the end of the play, he had a lot of free time during practice. He spent as much of it as he could with Bran. That wasn't easy—the older boy was always off on some errand or another for Mr. Hening, or in an odd corner of the school practicing his lines with Bert or Debbie and Warren Briggs.

After two days, as Keith half-dozed in an uncomfortable wooden auditorium seat, Laura Birtonelli sat down beside him and leaned over to whisper, "Are you doing anything?"

"Not really. Why?"

"Well, I'm going to be in charge of costumes, and I need someone to help me go through what we have in the prop room. You're elected."

Keith shrugged. "Lead on."

They tiptoed backstage, and Laura showed him into the prop room. It was larger than Keith had expected, a room about ten feet by five, the concrete walls lined with grey metal shelves and racks for hanging clothes. In the center was an imposing table covered with an array of junk left over from past performances. There were battered easy chairs, two scarred and much-painted dressers, and even an elaborate chandelier hanging from a hook set into the ceiling.

"You start there," Laura said, pointing, "And I'll start in the other corner. Anything that might work in the play, put on the table."

It wasn't long before Keith found a ballerina outfit with a billowing skirt. Chuckling, he held it up for Laura's inspection. "Maybe Debbie could wear this." Debbie's character was a sweet woman in her late sixties.

Laura laughed. "Good idea. No, better yet, let's have Jerry wear it."

In spite of himself, Keith giggled at the image of well-muscled Jerry Todd in a tutu. Then Laura pulled out an outrageous pirate outfit in green and brown and red, and laughed harder. "For you, in the last scene."

"Avast, ye scurvy dogs!" Keith said, which made him laugh even harder. In no time, they had the entire cast outfitted in the most bizarre costumes they could find. Tears streamed down Keith's cheeks, and he felt weak from so much giggling.

The door opened, and through flowing tears Keith looked up to see Debbie Vovcenko leaning against the doorway, with Bert and Bran peering over her shoulders. Debbie gave a smile. "Well, well, what have we here? A little love interest in the prop room?"

Laura looked at Keith, he met her eyes, and the two of them broke up. The other three watched patiently, Bran struggling to keep his face impassive, until Laura held up the ballerina costume.

"For you," she gasped, pointing at Debbie.

Bran chuckled. Debbie snorted disapproval, then walked away.

Bert shook his head. "Now she'll tell everyone that she found the two of you alone in the prop room."

"She *did*," Keith said, and that set Laura to laughing so hard she was seized by a coughing fit. Bran pounded her on the back until she stopped, and then they showed him all their choices of costume.

Debbie was silent during the ride home. That night, Keith slept soundly, completely worn out.

It was the following night, Thursday, that Keith sat in the kitchen working on algebra problems while his mother read the evening paper and did needlepoint. A glass of milk, half drunk, was forgotten on the table before him; some soft music played on the radio. Suddenly the phone rang, and Keith jumped. He grinned sheepishly.

"Sorry, Mom. I was concentrating."

She smiled. "It's okay. Just a few more white hairs."

Without leaving his chair, Keith grabbed the phone. "Hello?"

"Hello. May I speak with Keith Graff"

"This is Keith."

"I thought so. My good man, you don't sound that different on the phone."

A little shiver touched Keith's stomach. "Bran?"

"The one and only. How are you doing, fella?"

"Pretty good. How about you?"

"Wrestling with math problems at the moment. So I thought I'd take a break and give you a call."

Keith pushed back his chair, stood up. "Hey, can you wait while I get to the other phone?"

"Sure."

Keith bounded up the stairs to his room, fell on his bed and reached for the phone with a trembling hand. Stop it, he told himself sternly. He picked up the receiver and then shouted down the stairs, "Okay, Mom."

There was a click as his mother hung up the kitchen extension.

"Okay, I'm back," Keith said. "So what are you doing? Homework?"

"Algebra." Keith wrinkled his nose. "Do you know anything about factoring polynomials?"

"I used to know all that, but I forgot it over the summer. If you're having trouble ask Bert sometime. He's a whiz at math." Bran chuckled. "He's the only reason I'm passing advanced algebra."

"Yeah, Bert's a strange guy."

"So are we all, kid. Hey, I didn't call just to pass the time."

"Oh?" What else could he say?

"No. I want to know if you're free tomorrow after practice. Debbie's having a kind of a cookout, and we thought you might be able to come along."

"A cookout? That sounds like fun."

"Yeah, the whole gang will be there."

"I'll have to check it out with my morn, but I'm pretty sure it'll be okay."

"Good. It will be nice having you there."

"Thanks." Then there was silence, only the distant muted sound of a busy signal way off in the distance on the phone lines. The quiet went on for several long seconds, then Bran gave a nervous little laugh. "Well, I guess that's why I called. I'll see you tomorrow right before play production."

"Okay." Keith didn't want to let Bran go, didn't want to release the phone. But he couldn't think of anything else to say. The boys were silent for a minute more, then Bran coughed.

"All right, then, I'll see you tomorrow. Bye."

"Bye."

There was a click, and then the hum and crackle of a dead line. Keith held the phone until the dial tone came back on, then settled it in its cradle.

His mother gave him permission to go to the cookout, and he finished up his homework without paying too much attention to it. He probably had one or two of the problems wrong, but for now he just couldn't concentrate that much.

That night, the wind rattling at the windows woke Keith up. His clock told him it was one-fifteen; moonlit shadows of trees danced in his room. It was warm and cozy under the covers, and he lay still for a while, just savoring the feeling of being between sleep and wakefulness.

Bran had called him. Bran wanted him at the cookout. And in the silver-spattered darkness, Keith's sleepy mind wove other versions of the phone conversation. Wait, Bran, don't hang up. I have to tell you that I'm glad you're my friend. I have to tell you, Bran, what it means to me to be accepted by you and your friends.

I have to tell you, Bran, that I think I love you.

Keith curled up in bed, sleepily ran his hands over his own shoulders, hugged himself tightly and imagined it was Bran.

Cookout. What would it be like? Maybe a game of football in waning light, then hot dogs half-burned on the grill. Then the whole group sitting around the coals with sticks and marshmallows, while the night grew colder. And sooner or later, they would huddle together to keep warm, and Keith would feel Bran's arms around him, would settle his head on his friend's shoulder...

Keith jerked awake, sat up in bed. There was only his lonely room, lit by moonglow and the bright green of his digital clock. And the wind shrieked outside.

Go to sleep, Keith. And dream something else. Shivering in his thin pajamas, Keith pulled the covers around himself and closed his eyes.

*

Keith wore his green shirt to school the next day. He waited, as usual, for Bran after drama class - when the older boy bounded into the drama room he threw a salute in Keith's direction. "Love that shirt," Bran said.

"Thanks. Have a good class."

"What kind of mood is Bob in?"

Keith smiled. His class had done improvised scenes; he liked them best. "A good mood."

Bran nodded. "See you at lunch."

"Right."

He managed to get to his German class and just slid into his seat when the bell rang. The teacher raised her eyebrows, but didn't say anything. Someday soon, Keith thought, he would be late for German. But the few words he exchanged with Bran between classes were the brightest spot of his morning, and he was willing to take the chance.

They were reading a story in German; Keith listened to his classmates read, one at a time, and let his mind drift. Bran liked his shirt. Bran had invited him to tonight's cookout. Yet Bran paid Keith little attention during play practice, and at lunch Keith was just one of the gang, everyone serving as background and audience for Bran's witty comments.

I shouldn't complain, Keith thought. Three weeks ago he never looked at me, and now I'm his friend. But....

But *what*, Keith?

When he reached this point in his musings, Frau Schneider called on him to read, and he turned his attention to his German book. It wasn't until the change of classes, when he plodded from German to algebra, that Keith had time to recapture his train of thought.

What do I want?

Pushing through crowded halls, he passed a boy and girl walking slowly with arms around one another. And he nodded to himself.

Bran treated him well, then turned around and virtually ignored him. And Keith didn't want to push things, didn't want to make a pest of himself.

I need to know how he feels about me.

Jane Larson from the lunch table was in Keith's algebra class; lately they'd taken to sitting next to one another and passing notes back and forth when they could get away with it. Today he greeted her and then took advantage of the few minutes before class started to ask, "Hey, I'm having trouble with something."

"What?"

"Well, figuring things out. I know that *you're* going with Rick Lederman, and Warren's been seeing Marcia What's-her-name. And Bert and Laura aren't seeing anybody. But what's the story with Bran and Debbie? Are they…?"

Jane glanced at the clock, then back to Keith. "I thought so too. But nobody's really sure. Debbie likes to date around, and she's likely to come up with the strangest people. And Bran… well, does anybody know what Bran's doing? Half the time he acts like Debbie's his girlfriend, and the other half he ignores her. I know I've talked to him a couple of times when she's not there, and he doesn't seem to have a high opinion of her."

Keith shook his head. "This is so confusing."

Jane laughed, patted him gently on the head. "Don't worry. You'll figure it all out." She paused, then whispered, "Don't answer if you don't want to, but are you and Laura really…an item? Debbie's been spreading it around that…."

"No." Keith said at once. "Don't get me wrong, I like Laura, but we're not…involved." And I'm not going to tell you, Jane, just *who* I'm interested in. I don't want to start trouble for him.

The teacher cleared his throat, and Keith looked up to see the man's eyes on him and Jane. He blushed, and opened his notebook to the chuckles of classmates.

After class Jane dashed off to the girls' room, and Keith went ahead to the lunchroom alone, his questions still unanswered.

Bran waved and called to him across the crowded cafeteria. When Keith reached the table, he found Albert and Laura sitting together, furiously studying a physics book while absently gulping down sandwiches. Bran sat on the back of his chair, his feet in the seat, and shook his head.

"Can you do something to cheer these two up?" he asked Keith.

"What's wrong?"

Laura looked at him over her glasses. "A major physics lab Monday, and you ask what's wrong."

Keith slid into an open seat, leaned across Bert. "So there's a physics lab. So what? What are they serving today?"

"Chicken."

Keith shuddered. "I'll eat my sandwich."

Bran put his hand on Keith's shoulder, gently pulled him back. "You don't understand the procedure here, my boy. Whenever there's a lab scheduled, Laura and Jane and Warren start having fits three days in advance. Then comes the day of the lab, and we have to supply them with french fries and oatmeal cookies until the panic dies. Then we gather together for an evening while everyone determines that their labs didn't work and there is no way to make the answers come out right. So Albert grabs his calculator and the textbook, and he mutters to himself in a corner while Laura and Jane go quietly catatonic. Finally Bert emerges, having made up the right answers—everyone copies from him, and the collapse of Western Civilization is postponed for another month." Bran wiped his hands on his jeans. "It's great fun to watch."

Laura gave a single theatrical laugh. "Ha! Last year in chemistry you were just as panicked as the rest of us."

"Yes, my dear, but you forget that I didn't take physics. So I'm an innocent bystander and can watch the rest of you make' fools of yourselves."

Keith looked at the physics book, at Bran, and at Laura. "How can I get in on this deal? I can never make things work right."

Bran groaned. "Not another one!"

Laura smiled. "You're invited, Keith." She chewed on the end of her pencil, frowned. "If we can find a place to get together. Lab reports are due Thursday, which means we ought to get them together Wednesday night. That's Mom's night for her book group, so my house is out."

"What about the library?" Keith suggested.

Bran shook his head. "No good. We got thrown out last year."

"Thrown out of the library?"

Albert pointed an accusing finger in Bran's direction.

"It was *not* me!" Bran protested. Then he grinned. "Well, okay, maybe 1 was a bit loud. They just don't understand high-spirited artistic types like me."

Keith chewed on his lower lip while Laura made some comment about "artistic, not autistic." Then be said, "I can see if my Mom will let me have everyone over…"

Bran clapped him on the back. "Good man."

Bert nodded in Bran's direction. "1£ it will help, we can make sure that Mr. Artistic here doesn't come. It would give your parents a little peace."

"Oh, Mom won't mind. She wants to meet everyone, anyhow. I'll ask her tonight, and let you all know Monday."

"Great." Bran jumped off his chair, tousled Keith's hair and patted Laura's bead. "Don't worry, everything will be all right in physics-land."

Keith went to the counter to buy some milk, feeling a warm happiness inside. This is what he bad been missing since he moved to Oak Grove—easy give-and-take with friends, a sense of belonging. That was important to a guy.

When he returned, Bran stopped him in mid-stride and walked around him. "Damn, that's a fine shirt. I really approve of that shirt."

Bran's own shirt was a western-cut cotton shirt with buttons down the front. Keith grinned. "I like yours too."

A mischievous sparkle entered Bran's eyes. "Wanna trade?"

"Trade?"

"Yeah, trade." Bran started undoing his shirt buttons. "We're about the same size. I'll bet it would fit."

"What, trade shirts, just like that?"

"For the day." Bran had almost all his buttons undone; he pulled his shirttail from his pants and finished unbuttoning.

Keith couldn't hold back a chuckle. "This is insane."

"Come on," Bran encouraged.

Keith shrugged. What the hell. "Okay." He pulled his shirt over his head at the same time Bran slipped out of his, and then they both stood bare-chested in the middle of the cafeteria.

Keith couldn't keep his eyes from Bran. Square shoulders, smooth chest just touched with a bit of fuzz, firm stomach with a tracing of darker fuzz that trailed away below Bran's belt-line —for a mad instant Keith felt a desire to reach out and touch his friend's bare skin, then he came to his senses and forced himself to look away. A blush briefly touched his cheeks, then mercifully went away.

He slipped into Bran's shirt. It was warm, and smelled faintly of something else, a fragrance that escaped him but that he knew he would always associate with Bran.

Buttoning up the shirt, he struggled to wipe a slaphappy grin off his face. He nodded appreciatively. "It looks good on you," he said to Bran.

"Yeah. A little tight, but I can live with that."

Keith's green pullover made the lines of Bran's chest even more defined, hugged his shoulders and back just tightly enough to accent muscles beneath. Standing next to Bran, Keith felt pale, skinny and weak.

Laura shook her head, rubbed her eyes. "You guys will do *anything*."

Bran dimpled. "*You* want to trade now?"

"No." Laura clutched at her yellow knit top, then warily lowered her hands while Bran laughed. "I ought to take you up on that offer. Just to see what you'd do."

"Too late. I only trade shirts once a day. Keith filled my quota." He sat down, pulled a book from his vinyl knapsack. "Now everyone be quiet, I have to read a chapter before biology class." He looked around the table and beyond, where students were giving him odd looks while trying to pretend that they hadn't noticed the shirt-switching. "Sheesh!" Bran said. "All this noise, a fellow can't get anything done."

Keith laughed and turned his attention to his lunch.

The rest of the day, Bran's shirt was a comforting presence, like a friendly familiar blanket on a cold night.

If only...if only it could be Bran himself.

*

On stage that afternoon, Keith could do no wrong. He nearly forgot that it was only rehearsal, almost forgot that it was a play. He *was* Mr. Witherspoon, and he played the elderly gentleman with energy and confidence that he hadn't known he had in him. When he came down from the stage after his scene, Bert congratulated him and Bran slapped him vigorously on the back.

"A great job, Keith," Bran said. "Wonderful. I knew you could do it."

"I don't know," Keith said, embarrassed to be getting such praise from the senior class's best actor. He grinned. "Maybe it was the shirt. A little of your talent robbed off on me."

"Can't be," Bert said drily, "Bran doesn't *have* any talent."

Bran put his arm on Keith's shoulder and looked directly into the younger boy's eyes. And Keith suddenly knew that Bran was completely serious; he felt that Bran's manic personality had parted like a curtain to allow a brief glimpse of the young man who lay beneath. "You did good, Keith. Really."

Hoping that his tone conveyed his own seriousness and gratitude, Keith nodded. "Thanks. Thanks a lot."

Then Bran's curtain closed once more and he threw out his arms to embrace the whole cast. "Come on, let's get to Debbie's for the cookout."

Debbie at once scampered into the circle of Bran's arms, and he casually draped his right arm around her shoulders while she encircled his waist with her left. Following them up the aisle, Keith felt strangely at peace.

He walks like that with her. But I've never heard him tell her that *she* did good. Bran revealed something to me, that he doesn't show often.

And what did that mean?

Keith shook his head, dismissed the question, and followed the others to Bran's car.

CHAPTER FOUR

Seven people fit into Bran's old Plymouth. Debbie sat between Bran and Warren in the front seat, and Keith, Laura, Bert and Jane crowded into the back. Keith sat beside Laura, and in the gathering darkness he watched the play of early-evening headlights on Bran's face, in the boy's dark hair. This was a magical night, Keith thought—had been an unusual, magical day. Maybe it was Bran's shirt, still enclosing him like a warm friendly hug; maybe it was just leftover excitement from having done so well in rehearsal.

Keith felt almost as if he were standing outside his own body, watching himself the way he sometimes did in dreams. This isn't Keith Graff, he thought. Not the Keith Graff who was so miserable and lonely three weeks ago. Not this laughing, cheerful boy crammed between Laura Birtonelli and the car door. lm someone else now. I don't know who.

Whomever I am, I think I like him.

Bran looked in the rearview mirror, caught Keith's eye by accident and winked.

And *he's* the cause of this change, Keith thought. If I'm something I wasn't, Bran Davenport is the reason.

Debbie Vovcenko's house sat at the end of a dead-end road, on the edge of what looked like a deep woods. As the car stopped and everyone piled out, Keith smelled the homey fragrance of a charcoal fire, and below that he whiffed the scent of old trees, years upon years of fallen leaves, a slightly musty odor that he associated with Kinwood and long walks through the woods with his friend Frank.

I thought I'd never smell this again without feeling bad.

Keith shook his head and followed everyone into the house.

Debbie's house was pretty, the sort of house that was photographed in those decorator magazines that Mom read. Except somehow Mom never managed to make Keith's house look that way. And from the way Debbie and everyone else walked gingerly through the living room, Keith suspected that it was a good thing.

He was introduced to Mr. and Mrs. Vovcenko, and did his best to be courteous. He always felt funny meeting other people's parents. You never knew when parents really liked you, and when they were just putting up with you because you were their daughter's friend. Keith never knew what to say to someone else's parents.

I wonder how Mom will feel about these people I've become friends with?

"I can put the hot dogs and hamburgers on any time you want," Mr. Vovcenko said to Debbie. "Why don't you and your friends get the rolls and things out?"

Bran gave another of his smiles. "Don't worry about it, Mr. Richard. We'll take care of everything. If you'll show me where the meat is, I'll put it on the grill."

Debbie's father nodded, went to the refrigerator and took out a platter filled with hot dogs and raw hamburger patties. "The grill is ready for you. Thanks a lot, Bran." He saluted. "I leave things in your capable hands."

"You kids have fun," Debbie's mother said.

Debbie led everyone through the kitchen and out the back door. A large backyard grill was set up next to a redwood picnic table; a few lawn chairs were scattered about the large back yard. The woods began about twenty feet from the house, tall oak trees aflame with the colors of autumn, and tangles of small bushes retreating into the darkness. Debbie closed a switch on the brick wall of the house, and floodlights came on with a sudden flash of brightness.

"Laura, Jane, come on," Debbie said. "Let's get the rolls and stuff."

"Can we help?" Keith offered.

"You guys stay here and start the food cooking." The girls vanished into the house, and Keith wandered to the edge of the woods. Up in the treetops an autumn wind danced, rustling leaves and sending down a shower of acorns.

"Watch it," Warren said, helping Bran throw burgers on the grill. "Killer acorns."

"How many people are going to be here?" Bran called out to no one in particular.

Bert grunted. "Just us. The rest of the cast couldn't make it."

"Thank god," Warren said. "Or did anyone really want Susan Majors and the whole cheerleading squad here?"

Bert sat down at the picnic table, to all appearances ready to eat as soon as food was placed in front of him. "I have to confess, I've never really understood the attraction. What's she got that's so special?"

Warren slapped Bert on the back. "If you don't know, kid, then I feel sorry for you."

"Okay, so she's top-heavy. I keep expecting her to tip over when she walks. But other than that, what has she got?"

Warren considered. "Her face ain't that bad."

"My German shepherd's face isn't that bad either," Bert replied. "Besides, you can't have her face without having her open her mouth. And as far as I'm concerned, as soon as she talks she turns me right off."

"I agree. Cindy Banning, though, now *there's* a girl."

"Well, of course," Bert answered.

As the discussion went on, Keith glanced at Bran. The older boy gave a half-smile, and rolled his eyes.

The shirt, the warmth within him, the chill of the night and the feeling of possibilities all emboldened Keith. He walked over to where Bran stood, and in a low voice said, "What's the matter, don't you agree about Cindy Banning?"

Bran became suddenly interested in the burgers. "Let's just say she's not my type."

"Okay, let's say that." Keith tried to leave a question in his voice, but found he couldn't pursue the point.

"What about you?" Bran asked, cocking his head.

"Me? I don't even know the girl. I've seen her in the halls, that's all."

"What about you and Laura? Are you two really getting it on?"

Keith felt a touch defensive. "What makes you think that?"

"She's been awfully close to you in the last few days. That's all. It's none of my business, really."

"No, it is." Keith realized he was wringing his hands; he forced them apart and stuffed them into his pockets. "Laura's okay, I like her and everything...but not as a girlfriend."

"Is she pushing herself on you? If it bothers you, I could ask Debbie to have a talk with her."

"No." His reply was quick and automatic. "Don't do that. I don't think she's interested in me that way. Laura's just a nice, friendly person. She's trying to make me feel welcome."

Bran shrugged. "It's your own business."

At that point the girls returned, and for a few hectic minutes everyone was busy unloading rolls, mustard, ketchup, pickles, paper plates, and bottles of soda. Soon enough, the first of the hot dogs and hamburgers were ready, and the kids all sat around the table chewing away. Bran jumped up every few seconds to tend the fire, but otherwise it was rather peaceful.

"So," Keith said, to make conversation, "how do you all think the play is coming?"

Debbie ripped open a bag of potato chips and offered them around. "Not too bad, I say. It seems to be coming together a lot earlier than last year's play. If only Jerry can start remembering his lines I tell you, it's murder being up there waiting for him to pick up his cues."

"Yeah," Bran said, "it's better than last year. With the seniors gone, we can get things done without them being in the way." He frowned. "Keith, you're lucky you never saw last year's senior class try to act. They were the most pathetic bunch of no-talent stage-hogs I've ever run into."

"Remember when Sandy fell off the chair in dress rehearsal?" Laura said, laughing. Everyone else chuckled as she threw up her arms and took a dive to the ground, whooping as she went.

"And...and Dave forgetting his lines in One-Acts, so they had to put a prompter right behind the curtain?" Jane said, wiping her eyes.

"This is the best," Debbie said, holding up a hand. "When Andy took his earache medicine right before the opening night of 'Harvey', and started hallucinating in the middle of the first act."

"I could have killed him," Bran said, making a strangling gesture. "Warren, you saved that show. Once you got Andy back on track, he was able to carry on—but in the middle there, I thought we were going to lose everything."

"As it was," Laura explained to Keith, "we *did* lose about a third of the first act. We had to work in some of the best bits in the second act. Bob was going crazy, moving pages around in his playbook." She sat back. "I never felt so much like a professional as that night. Ladies and gentlemen, I think we deserve congratulations for saving that play."

"Hear hear!" Bran raised his coke bottle, and the other followed suit.

"So you think the play'll be okay?" Keith asked.

"No question," Bran answered. "Especially with you as part of the team. Folks, let's toast our newest star. To Keith!"

There was another toast, and Keith spread his arms and nodded acceptance. "I'd like to thank all the little people who made this honor possible,' he started, and was hooted down by the others.

"Who wants another hot dog?" Bran asked, jumping to the grill to rescue the food from cremation.

When everything was consumed, Debbie produced a package of marshmallows and the seven students crowded around the grill with sticks picked up from the yard. Keith found himself between Laura and Bran, feeling very relaxed and a little sleepy. As talk drifted around the circle, he let his mind wander.

How wonderful these people were. Talented, serious about what they were doing. And they accepted him, made him a part of their group. A boy has to have friends, he thought. You go mad if you don't.

And what about Bran? Right now, the older boy was staring intently at his marshmallow, watching lest the little ball of sugary fluff catch fire and be burnt to a crisp. What was Bran thinking?

A person had to have friends, sure. But more than that, you needed someone to be a special friend. Someone...well, someone to be what Frank had been for Keith. And more.

But what did Bran need?

Do I stand a chance? His expression when Bert and Warren were talking about the cheerleaders—what did that mean? Does Bran like girls?

Even as he framed the thought, Bran slipped his arm around Debbie and she laid her head on his shoulder.

Keith looked away. He doesn't know, can't know, that he bothers me when he does that. *I* want to be in her position. And I can't tell him. Not without jeopardizing our friendship.

Oh, there were plenty of boys at Oak Grove who were in love with other boys. Nobody minded...it was a concern of only the two boys involved. Dale Sullivan and Mark Greenberg, for example—both had parts in the play, and as far as Keith could tell, they had been a steady couple since junior high. Nobody looked twice at them.

But still...Keith couldn't tell Bran how he felt, not if it would make Bran uneasy. Better to keep his feelings to himself.

"I know what we can do," Laura said in a small voice.

"What?"

She backed away, leaving a hole in the circle open to the growing chill of the night. "Sensitivity exercises."

"Good idea," Jane said.

Keith furrowed his brow. "What are sensitivity exercises?"

Bran let go of Debbie. "You mean Bob hasn't had your class do sensitivity games yet? I'm surprised." He looked around the circle. "Folks, we have a sacrifice."

"Sacrifice?" Keith echoed. "This isn't going to hurt, is it?"

"Trust me."

Laura dug in a pocket, produced a red bandana. "Keith, we're going to blindfold you."

"What for?"

Bran said, "The whole purpose of these exercises is to get you in touch with your body and your senses. As an actor, you have to know your tools—and your body is your major tool." He sounded as if he were quoting from a textbook.

Warren snorted. "You do that better than Hening does."

"I've had more practice."

Laura held the bandana before Keith. "Are you game?"

"Don't feel pressured," Bran said, close to Keith. "It won't hurt. We've all done this kind of thing at one time or another, and I think everybody has liked it. But if you don't want to..."

Bert nodded. "Give it a try."

Keith shrugged. "Okay."

When the blindfold was firmly around his head, Keith felt strange. He touched the bandana, just to reassure himself that it was really there.

Bran seemed to read his mind. "Any time you want, you can take it off. We won't stop you. So don't worry."

"I'm not worried. What do we do now?"

There was a giggle, quickly stifled. Keith felt hands on his own, felt someone trace the shape of his fingers and turn his right hand palm-up.

"Who's that?"

"Just me," Bran answered comfortingly. "Now listen. We're going to give you a couple of objects—nothing sharp, nothing hot, nothing disgusting. We just want you to feel them, and then try to tell us what you're holding."

"O-okay."

The first was easy. "Hot dog roll," Keith said at once.

"Right. Try this."

The next object was cold, smooth, and strangely heavy. He tipped it, and his hands were touched by what felt like sand.

"Saltshaker!"

"Exactly." The saltshaker was removed, and replaced by a fuzzy object. "A sweater?" No, the texture was wrong. "A blanket."

"Close enough," Debbie said. "It's an old rug that my mother had hanging on the line."

"Here," Laura said. "Put your hands on this." She guided Keith a few steps forward, turned him, helped him stretch out his hands. He encountered something warm and fuzzy. "A dog?"

"No. But close."

He moved his hands, encountered ears, a face... "Somebody's head."

"Whose?" Laura asked.

The hair was short, there was fuzz on the chin...then Keith touched a familiar pullover shirt, and smiled. "Bran."

"Right," the older boy said, disentangling himself from Keith's hands.

Keith shook now, with excitement and nervousness. This was a new experience. Deprived of his sight, the whole world was different. Was this how blind people perceived things?

One thing was sure, he would never take texture for granted again. Forever after, his fingers would be far more sensitive to the things he touched in the course of everyday life.

Keith felt a steadying hand on his right arm, a warm body next to him. "Come with me," Bran said.

"Where are e going?" Keith asked, rooted to the spot.

"This is called a Trust Walk. I'll be your eyes. Just try to respond to me. I won't talk unless I have to. But I won't let you get hurt."

For the next ten minutes Keith let Bran guide him around the back yard. At first Bran had to talk quite a bit: "Take a step up," "Turn left," "Walk forward very slowly." But as the Trust Walk went on, Keith found that he picked up subtle bodily messages from Bran. A slight pressure to the left, and he turned; a minute hesitation and he stopped; a feather touch on his left knee and he lifted his leg.

His world was the back yard and the edge of the woods, and Keith was amazed at how broad and varied that world was. Trees—he reached out and ran his bare hands over the trees, feeling the roughness of the bark at the same time he smelled the sweet fragrance of living wood. Bran let him kneel down and swirl his hands in the ice-cold water in the goldfish pond; the shock of encountering wetness instead of the ground was invigorating and deliciously surprising.

"You've done this a lot," Keith said.

"I have," Bran answered softly. "Sensitivity and trust exercises are important to an actor. When we were doing *Harvey*, Bob had us run back and forth across the stage, blindfolded. Most of us got so good at it that we could stop within a foot or two of the edge of the curtain."

"Wow."

Keith felt Bran signal a stop, was aware of a sudden body ahead of him.

"Don't do that," Bran said, a touch of anger in his voice. "He can't see you coming, you know. You could hurt the guy."

"We're bored," Debbie's petulant voice said. "Can't we do something else?"

Keith took off the blindfold. The return of light to his eyes was dazzling. What a very strange experience.

This had been a day for new and strange experiences.

"I'm worn out," Keith said. "This is great, but it takes a lot of concentration. Is there something that everyone can join in with?"

Bran nodded. "What do you think, Laura? Person-in-the-middle?"

"Yes," Laura said gleefully. "I love it."

"What is it?" Keith asked.

Bran waved everyone into a circle. "Stand tight around me." When he was surrounded by all six, he directed, "Now everyone take half a step backward."

Bran was in the center of a rough circle now, facing Laura. He held out his hand to Keith. "The blindfold, please."

Keith handed it over, and Laura tied it around Bran's eyes. Then Bran stood straight, and took a breath.

"I'm going to pretend," he said, "that someone has nailed my feet to the ground. But there's no strength in my ankles. So I'll just fall this way and that." He started to fall backwards, and Warren caught him under the arms, stood him up again in the middle of the circle. "And I'll just keep falling until we decide to try the next victim."

A flash of tension ran around the circle, and then Bran fell.

To Keith the game was exhilarating and scary both at the same time. Laura on his right and Jane on his left both helped him when Bran started falling in his direction. There was one bad instant when Bran fell toward Debbie and she couldn't hold him, but Bert and Warren stepped in at once to help her and a nasty tumble was avoided.

Keith found that his muscles were tight and ready, his senses unusually acute. Bran had placed his trust in them all, and it was Keith's responsibility to do his part to see that that trust wasn't betrayed. He hardly had time to be conscious of the fact that he held Bran's body between his hands; he just caught the older boy, put him back up in the center, and waited for the next fall.

At long last, Bran stood straight up and ripped off the blindfold. The wave of relief that ran around the circle was almost as real as the chilly autumn breeze. "Who wants to go next?" Bran said.

Keith swallowed. "Can I try?"

"Don't feel pressured," Laura smiled. "If you want somebody else to go before you, that's fine."

"No, I want to try." He looked around the circle, opened his mouth. "Just don't—"

Bran silenced him with a finger on his lips. "We won't drop you. We've all been through this before. You can trust us, Keith."

The first time he fell, Keith stumbled and caught himself just as firm hands reached to steady him. He grinned sheepishly. "Okay, I trust you, it's just going to take a few times to get used to this."

"Take your time," Bran said.

The second time, Keith was able to fall without catching himself. From beyond the darkness of the blindfold, he felt hands on his chest and shoulders, hands that steadied him and supported him the way he'd supported Bran. He was placed back in the center of the circle, and he let himself fall backwards. Again the hands were there, strong and supporting.

Keith came to like the feeling. He was light, light as a windborne leaf. And the wind that upheld him was the arms and hands of his classmates, his friends. There was nothing to fear, now or ever—these people cared for him, they wouldn't let him fall and hurt himself. Keith relaxed, let his body grow heavy and limp.

Finally, he fell toward Bran; the older boy caught him, and then kept moving downward…until Keith lay on the cold ground, his head and shoulders cradled in Bran's arms, the others gathered around him. Bran took the blindfold from his eyes gingerly.

"I thought you fell asleep," Bran said. "Boy, you were really getting into it."

"It's great." Keith couldn't hold back a delighted smile. "I had fun."

Bran pushed him up, then stood. "Who's next?"

"Me in the middle," Laura said. She took the center point and the circle closed about her. Keith stood right next to Bran; together they kept Laura from falling each time she moved in their direction.

We make a good team, Keith thought.

Then Laura stopped, and took off her blindfold. "Group hug!" she shouted.

The circle closed around little Laura. Bran threw his arms around Keith on one side, Bert on the other; Keith himself snaked one arm behind Bran and stretched another across Jane's shoulders to clasp hands with Warren. The circle tightened, faces pressed together, arms intertwined more tightly. It was warm in the circle, warm despite the cold wind that rustled through the trees; Keith shivered, and the others held on even tighter than before.

Keith was acutely conscious of Bran's cheek pressed up against his own. The strength of his embrace was matched by a tightness in his groin and a strong feeling in the pit of his stomach.

I could kiss him right now, Keith thought. And then forever after, Bran would be on his guard.

No. I will just enjoy what I have, without wanting more.

But how long can I go on this way?

CHAPTER FIVE

The cookout was Friday night; for the rest of the weekend Keith was busy. his mother gave him permission to host the physics lab brainstorming session, but she decreed that the house must be cleaned before visitors arrived. So all day Saturday and Sunday she and Keith scrubbed, vacuumed, washed clothes, and laid in enough cokes, potato chips, and frozen pizzas to satisfy even a regiment of high school students. In between all this activity, Keith even managed to locate the box with Halloween decorations, and by Sunday night the house was hung with goblins, witches, and a lifesize glow-in-the-dark skeleton on the door.

As Keith and his mother worked toward one another form opposite ends of the kitchen floor, each scrubbing furiously, she sighed. "I'm glad you're having folks over, or this floor might never get done."

Keith laughed.

"So tell me about these people," his mother went on. "At least I'll have some idea of who they are when I meet them."

"Well, I'm still not sure who's going to be coming. Jane, she's in my algebra class. Debbie, she seems a little stuck-up but once you get underneath that she's really pleasant. Bert is sort of a nerd, I guess. A nice guy, though. Then there's Warren…he's all-American, the typical senior—you'll probably like him best."

"I'll make up my own mind."

"And Laura, she's neat. She's too shy for her own good sometimes." Keith sloshed more warm sudsy water on the floor, attacked a patch of dirt with his scrub-brush. "But once you get to know her, you realize that she doesn't have a mean bone in her body."

"Is she your girl?" Mom asked, her voice completely neutral.

Keith flushed. "No. We're friends, that's all."

"It's all right to tell your mother to mind her own business. I'm not trying to pry, I just want to be able to know your friends. You've been so happy since you got involved in the play."

"Oh, I know. Laura and I   just aren't involved." He frowned. "It's a little hard to figure out who's involved with whom in this group."

"You'll get it all settled. Anybody else I should know about? How about the fellow playing Teddy? Will he be here?"

"Bran?" Keith smiled. "He should be. I hope you'll like him. He's got kind of an excited personality, but it's pretty much all for show. Underneath he's just as serious and you and I. He gets straight A's, but you wouldn't know it to look at him."

"He's your best friend, then?" Again, Mom's voice held no emotion. It was just an interested question.

Keith considered. "No, I wouldn't say that. I think Frank is still my best friend." Except that Frank's last letter was still unanswered on Keith's desk, and he hadn't talked to Frank on the phone for two weeks.

I've been busy, Keith thought.

"Do you miss Kinwood the way you did when we first moved?"

"I don't think so, Mom. Oh, sure, i wonder about what the kids at school are doing, what play they're working on this year. They were talking about *Cabaret* this summer." He shook his head. "And I guess all the little kids in the neighborhood are getting ready for trick-or-treating. I'll miss that, too."

"There'll be trick-or-treating here."

"I know." Keith had finished his section of floor; he took his bucket to the sink and started to dump it, slowly so that he wouldn't overload the drain. "And now I've got friends, I don't feel so lonely at school." He took his mother's bucket from her, and dumped it too. "It's important to belong."

"Just don't put too much importance on belonging, Keith. Make sure you do things because *you* want to, not because the group wants you to."

"You mean like drugs, and that sort of thing? Don't worry, Mom, we're not into that." The gang was hard enough on the poor guy who took his earache medicine before a performance and started hallucinating onstage—he could imagine what they would do to someone who used illegal drugs. Probably kick them out of the cast, or at least make their life pretty miserable while they stayed.

"That, too," Mom said. "Also life in general. Don't let the crowd pressure you into doing anything you don't want to—or giving up something you do want. It's your life, son, not anybody else's."

Keith shivered, and wondered suddenly if his mother knew how he felt about Bran, about the uncertainties that haunted his thoughts. Was she telling him in a roundabout way to pay less attention to what the gang would think, and more to what he wanted?

He shrugged. It was so hard to tell, with parents. Mom, especially. He still didn't know if she understood what had been going on with Frank. When they first moved, Keith was sure she did know, and that she was taking him away just to separate him from Frank. After a few days he had come to his senses, and decided that she didn't know anything.

As she struggled up off the floor, Keith gave her a hand, then hugged her briefly. "Anyway," he said, "thanks for letting me have everyone over." He hesitated. "And thanks for the advice. Thanks for caring."

She squeezed his shoulder. "I always do."

*

Physics was Keith's first class of the day. Monday morning
he started his lab experiment, a demanding task that involved
precise measurement of various weights sliding down an
incline. It wasn't his favorite of the experiments they'd done...
he liked the one with the pendulum a lot better. And he
couldn't keep his mind on his work; he kept thinking back to
Friday night and the wonderful feeling of unity he had shared
with the others.

Between drama and German, he waited as usual for Bran
to arrive at the drama room. The older boy didn't show up
right away, although Keith did say hello to Bert and Debbie on
their way in. After waiting almost the full five minutes of
between-class time Keith dashed toward German. Halfway
there he passed Bran, also rushing. Bran spun and gave Keith
an apologetic wave. "Hope you're not too late to class, kid. I'm
real sorry. I was bullshitting with Warren after history and
time got away from me."

"Hey, it's okay. See you at lunch."

"Okay. Sorry again." Then Bran was gone, and Keith just
managed to get to class as the bell was ringing.

At lunch Keith found himself very popular, as everyone
but Bran asked him questions about the physics lab.

"Don't worry about it," Keith said. "It's not that hard to
do, just be careful with observations. Make sure you get
everything down as accurately as you can."

"Half of last year's seniors got D's on this lab," Debbie
said. "It's supposed to be a real killer."

Keith shook his head. "It's all gravity. How can you get
gravity wrong?"

"I don't think," Laura said, "that the laws of nature apply
in our classroom. We *never* get labs right."

Bran snorted. "And Bert always fudges the figures so that
nobody gets a bad grade. What are you all so upset about?
Jeez, you'd think this lousy physics lab was the Nobel Prize or

something." He sounded more irritated than Keith had ever heard him, and Keith had a sudden flash of intuition.

Bran feels left out, he thought. Everyone is involved in this lab except him, and he doesn't like not being a part of things. Not any more than the rest of us do.

"Hey, there's no reason you can't grumble along with the rest of us," Keith said. "You're an honorary part of the class anyhow." He smiled. "Skip algebra one morning and come to physics with me. Come tomorrow and you can help me finish the lab."

Debbie gave Keith a cold glance. "I'm sure Bran would rather come to class with the *rest* of us."

Bran scowled. "I'm not going to anybody's physics class. I'm sick and tired of hearing about physics. Why doesn't somebody decide to have a fit about the algebra test next week?"

"Give us time," Laura said. Everyone laughed except Bran, who rolled his eyes.

When the bell rang to end lunch period, Keith caught up with Bran and walked beside him. "Hey, Bran, you okay?"

"I'm fine," Bran said with a sigh. "It's just that I'm tired of having everybody get so serious about this lab thing. It's no big deal."

"You're still coming to my house for the lab report, aren't you?"

"I don't know. Probably. Here's my class. See you at rehearsal."

Keith walked on alone to his history class, a lump in his throat. "Probably?"

Suppose he didn't show up?

No matter. Keith would still have fun. He didn't need Bran to enjoy the company of his new friends. Cripes, he thought, I'm not *that* far gone. I can still enjoy life without having him around all the time.

And yet….

If he doesn't show up, I'm going to be disappointed.

*

Bran's outburst seemed quite forgotten by the time play rehearsal started. Mr. Hening spent most of the time working on scenes involving Debbie, Jane, and Jerry Todd—so Keith had plenty of time to sit up in the lighting deck and whisper with Bran.

"Debbie and Jane work together well," Keith observed, looking down at the stage.

"Yeah," Bran agreed. "Jerry's the problem. He's got his mind on too many things. He's not paying attention to what he's doing." Bran pounded softly on the lighting board. "He's going to wreck the play if he doesn't buckle down and get to work."

"He will."

"He'd better. Less than three weeks to go. I thought Jerry had the ability to do this part. Look at him—he's standing like a statue. We're going to have to do something to get him loosened up."

"How about sensitivity exercises?" Keith suggested.

"That's not such a bad idea." Bran looked at Keith, and his eyes softened. "Well, nothing we can do about it right now. Bob is going to help him more than we can, at this point."

Keith was seated in one of the two chairs before the board; Bran sat down in the other and moved it to face Keith. "You want to try another one of those exercises?"

"Sure."

"Okay, here it is. We look at each other—that's it. Just stare into one another's eyes, without saying a word."

Keith couldn't help a giggle. It sounded so silly. "All right, I'm ready to give it a try."

"Okay. Now."

Bran set his hands lightly in his lap, and looked steadily at Keith. For the first few minutes Keith felt very uncomfortable; he stifled a few laughs, and had to look away once or twice.

Then, gradually, calm descended upon him and he found himself able to look into Bran's face without feeling nervous.

Even in the half-darkness of the lighting deck, Keith was able to see the light brown of Bran's eyes, and the pattern of stage lights reflected in them. He let his eyes travel over his friend's face, noticed the slight tilt of Bran's head and the movement of nostrils when he breathed.

Bran, do you know how I feel about you? This is only the second time I've had a glimpse of the Bran that you hide from everyone, the serious young man beneath the exuberant boy… and already I'm in love with that person.

Keith's arm twitched involuntarily, and Bran's hard, serious expression softened just a trifle.

Like when we were doing that trust walk, Keith thought. Bran, I'm starting to read even your most minor movements. We're communicating, somehow, even though we aren't saying a word.

But what is he trying to say?

As more time passed, Keith's troubled mind settled and he passed beyond such questions. There was only the present, the dimness and Bran's face, and he didn't look beyond to find any meanings. He didn't worry about the future. He was with his friend, and that was enough.

I will remember this moment for the rest of my life.

Bran.

Keith shifted in his chair, moved his hands forward on his lap. And Bran glanced down, then lifted his own hands and placed them over Keith's. The warm touch of Bran's palms on the back of his hands was a shock to Keith, and he shivered.

He opened his mouth, but Bran gave a tiny shake of his head. No. Don't talk.

For a long minute Keith sat completely still, his hands covered by Bran's. Then he turned his wrists, met Bran's hands palm-to-and touched Bran's fingers tenderly.

Bran sighed, then suddenly took his hands away. He turned his head, breaking the spell.

"Sorry, kid," Bran whispered.

"What's wrong?"

"Don't panic. I'm just not in the right mood."

What was happening? Was it something Keith had done? Had he acted too quickly, done too much?

"Bran...is something the matter? Can I do anything?"

"No. Just a mood. It's...personal."

Keith wanted to shake Bran, to say "Tell me, tell me what's going on." But he had to respect his friend's privacy.

"Okay," he said dubiously. "If you want to talk about it, I'm here. I'll listen."

"Thanks," Bran said, gripping Keith's shoulder for a second. "Come on, let's go down and sit with the others."

Keith followed Bran down the ladder, his mind in turmoil. What had he done?

*

Tuesday passed without anything particularly interesting happening. Laura brought homemade cookies in for lunch, and shared them with everyone; after play practice Bran dropped Keith off at home and said his customary goodbye. But Keith had a feeling deep within that something was not right, that he had done too much with Bran, had pushed a moment of intimacy too far.

"What time are your friends coming tomorrow?"

"Huh?" Keith looked up from his dinner, which he'd hardly noticed, and saw his mother staring at him. "I'm sorry, Mom. If it's okay, everybody'll be coming here right after practice. About the usual time. Five thirty?" Keith guessed.

"I'll wait until everybody's here to put the pizzas in the oven, then."

"Okay, that's fine." Keith poked at his plate with his fork.

"You're not getting sick, are you?"

Keith forced a smile. "No, just distracted. Schoolwork and all," he lied.

Mom nodded, and let the subject drop. That was one of the nice things about her, Keith thought: she didn't keep hammering at something when you just wanted to be left alone.

The next day, Keith rode the bus home right after school. He wasn't needed at rehearsal—they were practicing only the first act—and he thought he'd better be home to help make the last-minute arrangements for the physics brainstorming session.

It was chillier than usual during Keith's two-block walk from the bus stop. Late October—the day before Halloween— and already most of the trees had lost their leaves, except the hardy evergreens. Keith pulled his warm jacket around himself to keep out the wind, and soon let himself into the empty house.

His first order of business was a shower. Hot water warmed Keith through to his chilled bones. Hair still dripping, body wrapped in a towel, he stumbled into his room and started looking through his clothes. His eyes fell on Bran's shirt, casually draped over the desk where he'd left it Friday afternoon.

Feeling a little silly, Keith closed his eyes and rubbed the shirt against his cheek, as if by doing so he could make some kind of telepathic contact with Bran.

What have I done wrong, Bran? Am I driving you away?

He doesn't like boys, Keith thought. He's just being friendly, and Monday on the lighting deck he was trying to show me some more sensitivity exercises. He's so serious about acting, and all he wanted to do was to help me become a better actor.

And I betrayed him. Without permission, without his knowledge, I went beyond the bounds of our friendship.

Keith flushed. Bran *had* to know what was going on. That was why he was being so cool suddenly.

What am I going to do?

Keith curled up on his bed, pulled the covers over him and hugged Bran's shirt tightly. He felt as if he wanted to cry; but he held back tears and forced himself to calm down.

It's not the end of the world. So I made a move, and Bran knows I'm interested. At the same time, though, I know he's *not* interested. He let me know gently, without hurting my feelings too much.

Okay, then, I'll just have to remember not to do anything like that again.

Keith took a deep breath. "All right, Bran," he whispered into the still air, "I won't bother you. We can be just friends, I'm sure we can. You'll learn that you can trust me."

Keith lay still for a few more minutes, feeling very tired. Then he rose, folded Bran's shirt very neatly and laid it on the desk, and dried his hair. So he loved someone who didn't love him. So what? It happened to a lot of kids. He would grow out of it.

Wouldn't he?

*

As the evening came closer Keith tried not the watch the street, but half a dozen times in the hour between five and six he found himself drawn to the window at the sound of cars driving past. Finally he was rewarded by the sight of Laura Birtonelli's beat-up Gremlin. The car pulled up in front and out stepped Laura, Jane, Bert, and Jane's friend Rick Lederman.

Keith welcomed his friends and introduced them to his mother, who smiled sweetly and said hello. As he took their coats, he said, "Where's everybody else?"

"Debbie's coming by herself," Laura said. "Bran dropped us off at home after play practice and said he might not be able to make it. Warren's having car trouble, and I think the two of them are going to try to fix it."

"Oh." Keith felt a pang of disappointment, then forced himself to ignore it. He didn't need Bran Davenport around to have a good time with his friends!

He led everyone into the living room, encouraged them to settle around the coffee table. "Mom's going to put pizzas on— does everybody want something to drink?"

There was a chorus of "yeses" and Keith fetched drinks while everyone unpacked books, calculators, and pencils. Before they'd even begun to work on the lab the doorbell rang, and Keith jumped up to let Debbie in.

"Just pick a place and make yourself at home," he said. "Food will be here shortly."

"Good, I'm famished." Debbie threw her coat down on a chair and sat on the couch next to Rick and Jane—Laura and Bert were on the floor.

"Okay," Bert said, opening his notebook, "Let's get to work here. Debbie, Jane, Keith, let me see your lab results."

They handed over the results, and then the true brainstorming session began. Some of the results were useless— Keith's entire first and second trials were too far off the mark to be used in the lab report.

"Margolis lets us have up to ten percent error," Bert said. "It's better to have four or five. I've figured out the conditions for five percent error—I'll pass this sheet around and tell me if your results are anywhere near this."

By the time they'd settled on which results to use, the pizzas were ready. Munching happily, everyone did what they could to help Bert do computations. As each sheet was finished he passed it on, and soon everyone was furiously copying down numbers and equations.

"Isn't Mr. Margolis going to be suspicious when he sees that we all have the same numbers?" Keith asked.

Laura shook her head. "We worried about that last year in Chemistry. He's go a hundred and twelve of these things to grade, in a week. He won't pay any attention to any of the numbers."

"And even if he does," Bert said, looking up from his calculator, "he knows we fudge figures. That's the best way to learn how to handle the equations. So don't worry."

Keith shrugged, and stopped worrying.

Finally, at about nine-thirty, the lab was done. Keith laid back on the floor and stretched. "What a job. Thanks, Bert. You were wonderful."

"That was a bad one," Bert agreed. He looked around the room, his eyes seeming to focus for the first time in hours. "Jane, do you have your guitar?"

"It's out in the car."

"Bring it in," Rick Lederman encouraged. Keith sat up and joined in the urging. Jane went outside and returned a minute later with a black guitar case. She settled down on the floor and strummed the instrument.

Soon everyone was singing along as Jane played. She did mostly show tunes, things from other plays that Oak Grove had done or shows they'd seen. Keith knew many of the songs from Kinwood, and when he didn't he just hummed along. Even his mother joined in, sitting on the stairs and hanging back from the kids' gathering, but still obviously enjoying herself.

"How about some more pizza?" Mom offered when Jane took a break. She went off into the kitchen and Keith brought more drinks.

"I'm sorry Warren and Bran didn't show up," Laura said. "They don't know what they're missing."

"I hope Warren's car trouble isn't too bad," Rick said.

"Car trouble?" Debbie laughed. "Warren had to change his oil. He just didn't want to work on the lab."

"And someone will give the results to him," Bert said drily.

"And how come Bran is suddenly so interested in changing oil?" Jane asked. "Usually he doesn't even know where the gas goes in."

Debbie chuckled again. "Oh come *on*, Jane. Everybody knows that Bran has the hots for Warren. You honestly mean that you haven't been able to tell?"

Bert snorted. "I thought *you* had the hots for Warren, Deb."

Debbie twirled a few strands of her long hair. "Laugh if you want to. I think it's pathetic. Warren doesn't have any interest in that sort of thing. You remember how mad he got when Dale Sullivan tried last year." Her self-satisfied smile seemed to say that she knew firsthand about Warren's tastes.

Laura patted Debbie on the head. "You're just sore because Bran didn't tell you he wasn't coming tonight. You thought he was supposed to check in with you all the time, didn't you?" Something in Laura's manner softened the impact of her words —she seemed to be half-kidding.

"Right," Debbie said sarcastically. "I'm not ready to be tied down to one guy—I don't care *what* Bran does with his time." She looked around. "Matter of fact, it's been kind of nice not having him around for once." She looked at Bert. "What's going to be on the algebra test, now that we have the lab out of the way?"

Keith left the group talking about the upcoming algebra test, while he helped his mother in the kitchen. But he was so lost in thought, mulling over what Debbie had said, that he almost burned himself on hot pizza, and Mom sent him back to the living room with a concerned look.

Bran? Warren? Was Debbie telling the truth, or was she just gossiping? Keith thought back over the last few weeks, and couldn't make up his mind.

Probably not true, he thought.

Probably.

CHAPTER SIX

It was about ten-thirty when everyone left; Keith silently helped his mother straighten up the living room, moving automatically through the routine of clearing up plates, loading the dishwasher, throwing away crumpled pieces of paper.

"Your friends are very nice," Mom said at last. "Jane plays the guitar very well. It was good to hear some music again."

"I'll tell her you said so." Keith poured powdered soap into the dishwasher, closed the door and turned the machine on. "Thanks for letting me have everybody over."

"Your friends are always welcome." Mom looked steadily at him for a few seconds, then said, "Let's see. I met everyone except…what's his name…Bran?"

Keith nodded. "He's not in the physics class, so he didn't come over tonight. One of the other guys, Warren, needed help with his car, and I guess Bran helped him."

Keith turned away, and didn't see the concerned look that crossed his mother's face.

He took his books upstairs and looked over the lab report to make sure it was ready to be handed in tomorrow. Everything seemed to be there.

He heard a knock at the door, and raced to the stairs. Mom got there first, opened the door, and stepped back. Keith started downstairs, then stopped halfway.

Bran stood on the porch, his hair ruffled by the wind.

Keith just about flew down the stairs. "Bran," he said uselessly.

"Pleased to meet you, Bran," Keith's mother said. "Won't you come in?"

"Thank you," Bran answered with a mischievous grin. "Keith didn't tell me that he had a sister."

Mom smiled indulgently. "Aren't you a charmer?" She playfully batted Bran's head. "Get in here before you make an old woman catch pneumonia."

Bran, in his blue windbreaker, faced Keith. For a moment neither boy spoke. Then Keith nervously slapped his hands together, and said, "So, what brings you here?"

"I saw a light on and figured it would be okay to stop in. I wanted to apologize in person for not showing up tonight. Warren needed some help with his car, and to tell the truth I just couldn't face Debbie and Laura and all this anxiety about physics."

"Take your jacket off. Would you like something to eat? We have some pizza left, and there's cookies and milk."

"A cookie or two would be fine indeed," Bran said, shrugging off his jacket.

Keith's mother started up the stairs. "You boys go ahead and settle in the kitchen. I'm going to do a little work before I go to sleep, but you won't bother me."

Keith led Bran into the kitchen, sat the older boy down and put the cookie jar in front of him. He poured two glasses of milk, and then sat down across from Bran.

"Good cookies," Bran said around a mouthful. "You mom make 'em?"

"Uh-huh. I helped. We made them this weekend."

"You did a good job."

"I hope Warren's car doesn't have serious trouble," Keith said, with what he hoped was the proper noncommittal tone. Inwardly, his mind screamed questions to Bran: Why were you with Warren? What were the two of you doing?

"Mmm, Just an oil change...new filter, all that rot. Do you have a car?"

"I drive Mom's sometimes."

"Aw, you gotta get a car. Best thing that ever happened to me. You have no idea what it's like, kid—you're free to go anywhere you want, to do anything you can think of." There was a faraway gleam in Bran's eyes, and Keith had the feeling that the older boy was not completely in the kitchen.

"You like driving?"

"Love it. I've been driving around for about an hour now, after finishing up Warren's car. No place in particular, just driving around." Bran looked down, focused his eyes on his milk. "Anyway, like I say, I wanted to come by to let you know that it wasn't anything personal, tonight." Bran cocked his head and looked at Keith strangely, as if waiting to see how Keith would react to his statement.

And what does he want me to say? Suppose I ask him, why did you pull away from me on the lighting deck? Why have you been distant these past two days?

And why did you come by here tonight, rather than just calling or talking to me tomorrow in school?

Bran, don't you know what you're doing to me?

If Debbie's right—if you *do* like boys—then maybe I have a chance.

I don't want maybes.

For just an instant Keith felt ready to reach across the table to Bran, to give voice to all the thoughts seething within him. Then, before he could will his hands to move, he lost nerve and instead said, "Will Warren get the lab results all right?"

"After we got the car put back together, he was going to cruise over to Debbie's and try to copy the report from her. So I guess everything'll be okay."

"Good."

"Hey, these really are spectacular cookies."

"Have another."

Keith nibbled on a cookie of his own, and watched with approval as Bran devoured two more.

"You can make cookies for me anytime," Bran said.

"I'll have to invite you over some time when we're making them, and you can help out. It's not that difficult."

Bran sighed. "It sounds like you and your Mom do a lot of things together."

Keith considered. "Yeah, Mom and I are awfully tight. My Dad is living in Texas with his second wife; I don't see him all that much. They were divorced about four, five years ago. Anyway, Mom and I have a lot of fun together."

"Must be nice." Bran took a sip of milk, wiped his mouth on his sleeve. "I live with my Dad—Mom died when I was fifteen. Since then, things haven't been really right with Dad."

"What's wrong?"

"Nothing in particular." Bran's normally cheerful face dropped into a neutral expression, and his eyes lost a little of their glimmer. "Oh, I guess he loves me and everything—but I think he's afraid to get too close. So I get a lot of things, like the car and a good allowance and all that...but Dad works late a lot of the time, and when he's home all he does is watch TV and read the paper. I don't like being at home alone."

"No brothers or sisters?"

"My brother's twenty-seven—he's married and lives in Seattle. I don't get to talk to him much." Bran shook his head. "I guess that's why my friends mean so much to me. And why I wanted to make sure that you knew I wasn't mad at you or anything."

Keith felt an overwhelming need to move, and instead of reaching out to take Bran's hand he stood up and carried his dirty glass to the sink. "Don't worry. I know you're not mad at me. I guess I can understand—I mean, it wouldn't be a whole lot of fun for me to sit in when you guys are studying for your algebra test."

Bran stood as well, brought his glass to the sink and handed it to Keith. "You understand a lot, you know that? I...I can talk to you like I can't really talk to the others. Maybe it's because you're new."

"Oh, I don't know," Keith said automatically. "The others are nice people."

"Don't get me wrong," Bran said, leaning against the counter and stretching his legs out in front of him. "They're fine. But talking to Bert is like carrying on a conversation with interstellar aliens, and Warren's idea of stimulating talk is discussing the Cowboys game last Sunday."

"How about Laura? She seems to be on the ball."

Bran regarded his running shoes. "Yeah, Laura's okay. Except she gets so damned worked up. The last time I told her the sad story of my life, she was in tears and all over me with sympathy. A fella can only take so much of that."

Keith nodded. "I know what you mean. There was this girl I knew at Kinwood, Brigette was her name. She was like that. Overreacted to everything. Once she set her sights on a friend of mine, and he said breaking up with her was like stabbing a knife in her chest." He didn't mention that the friend was Frank, or the long talks he and Frank had had about Brigette and other girls.

Or what their talks had led to.

"Hey," Bran said, looking at his watch, "It's getting late. I didn't mean to keep you up this long."

"Don't worry."

Bran straightened up, offered Keith his hand. "I'll see you tomorrow, kid."

Keith reached for Bran's hand, suddenly found that the older boy was gripping him on the right forearm, felt his own hand close naturally around Bran's forearm. Bran smiled. "That's the way the Romans used to shake hands. I saw it in a book. What do you think?"

Keith grinned. "I like it."

"Good." Bran tightened his grip, then let Keith's arm go. "Thanks for the cookies."

Watching Bran depart, Keith still felt phantom pressure of the older boy's grip on his arm.

Just when I thought I had you figured out, Bran Davenport, you breeze into my kitchen and start me wondering again. Damn it, what give you the *right*?!

Shrugging, Keith went upstairs.

*

The next day was Halloween. Riding the bus to school, Keith thought about being a little kid, and how much Halloween had meant to him then. He remembered a few of the truly great costumes he'd worn...the year he went as Captain Hook, the elaborate elephant costume that Mom had made when he was only eight. And all the candy! How had he managed to eat it all without getting sick? Little kids, he decided, have stomachs of steel. Nothing bothers them.

When the bus arrived he got off and wandered in the front door of the school. There, between the front office and the media center, he saw a large knot of people and pushed forward to see what they were looking at.

"Keith!" Laura was at his side, red-eyed and quaking with laughter. "Come here, you've *got* to see." She pulled him through the crowd.

Someone was dressed up in a flashy outfit of red and green, a jester's costume complete with little bells and fanciful makeup. Keith chuckled, then looked closer and saw that the actor was Bran.

He howled, reached for his friend's hand and shook it with violent approval. "I should have known," he said between gasps for breath. "Halloween, right?"

"Forsooth!" Bran said, grinning his widest grin. "Trick or treat?"

"I don't have any candy for you, little boy."

Bran raised his arms and pirouetted. "What do you think?"

"I love it. Where did you get this?"

"The basic costume is from a skit we did last year; I added the bells and a few flourishes myself."

Keith looked at all the kids who had gathered to chuckle at Bran's outfit. "Yeah, well, you've drawn quite a crowd. I have to hand it to you, Bran, yours is the best Halloween costume I've seen in a long time."

"Thanks." The first bell rang, and the people in the hall started to disperse. Bran waved his arms and made a jingle of bells. "Come on, Laura, we've got to get to class. See you later, Keith."

Keith shook his head. "Right. See you."

After Drama class Keith just managed a quick glimpse of Bran walking down the hall dogged by admirers, and then he had to run to German.

As soon as he got to algebra, his next class, Jane was waiting for him. "Did you see Bran?" she asked.

Keith smiled. "Isn't he something? I wish I'd thought of it myself."

Jane frowned. "I'm not so sure it's a good idea. At least, I heard Tony Ramierez talking last period; apparently that whole Student Government crowd isn't too happy with Bran showing up in costume."

Keith waved dismissal. "They're not happy about anything, unless they think of it first."

"I don't know," Jane said hesitantly. "If they decide to cut the budget of the Drama Club…"

"Oh for heaven's sake, that's the most ridiculous think I've ever heard."

Their discussion was ended by the beginning of class, and while the teacher went over homework problems, Keith fumed. Some people were so closed-minded, they couldn't accept anything new. Now if the Student Government had sponsored a Halloween Dress-Up Day, Tony Ramierez and his bunch would be happy to support it…but let it be Bran's idea, and all they could do was grumble.

Before class was properly started, there was a knock at the door and Keith saw Laura Birtonelli in the hall holding two yellow pass slips. She spoke with the teacher, who in turn beckoned Keith and Jane to the front of the room.

"What's up?" Keith said, puzzled.

Laura handed him a pass, gave the other to Jane. "Mr. Hening asked if you two could come down to the auditorium. Play business."

The math teacher smiled. "You guys understand what we're doing today, don't you?"

Keith and Jane nodded. Keith couldn't keep a puzzled expression off his face.

"Go on, then."

Out in the hall, Keith stopped and folded his arms across his chest. "What's this all about?"

Laura grabbed his hand, pulled him down the hall. Jane followed. "Very simple," Laura said over her shoulder. "Bran's miserable. We just passed him on the way to Drama." Laura and Warren had Drama Two right after Bran, Bert, and Debbie had Play Production. "Everyone is ribbing him something terrible, and the Student Government types are ready to string him up."

"What can we do?" Keith asked.

"Come with me." They arrived at the auditorium; Laura dug in her pocket and produced a key, opened the door. "Bob Hening wrote us passes and gave me the key. Warren will be here soon."

"What are we doing?"

Laura led them to the prop room. "Elementary, Keith my dear. We're all going to dress up, so Bran won't be the only one."

Keith smiled, then laughed, then hugged Laura and swung her around. "Great!"

In fifteen minutes they were all costumed—Keith wore the pirate outfit, Jane dressed in the ballerina costume, Laura wore a bridal gown and sequined mask, and Warren arrived just in time to slip into a Roman Centurion outfit left over from a one-act play far before anyone could remember.

"Now what?" Keith said, as they all stood on the stage lit by one lonely spotlight.

Laura looked at her watch. "Bran's in Creative Writing right now. I have a pass for him from Bob...what say we try to spring him?"

Keith grinned widely. "I love it. Let's go."

Outside the auditorium, they joined hands and skipped down the hall singing "We're off to see the Wizard." Keith found himself nearly lightheaded from the giddy madness of it all.

He tried to imagine himself back at Kinwood, doing this. Kinwood was a nice enough school, but he couldn't see himself breaking all the unwritten codes so easily. At Kinwood, people just didn't dance through the halls in costume, even if it *was* Halloween.

The Creative Writing teacher, a jolly fat woman, squealed and clapped her hands when the costumed troupe entered her room. "Kids, that's the best thing I've seen in ages. You're here for the jester—go ahead, take him."

Safe in the hall, armed with passes, the group paused. And Bran looked from one to the other, just shook his head.

"Thanks, all of you." He went from person to person, gave each a hug.

Keith, surprised and pleased, did his best to hug back as sincerely as he could.

They wound up giving a little impromptu skit in the cafeteria at lunch, and even Tony Ramierez and the Student Government table joined in the applause.

*

That evening at dinner, Keith told his mother the whole story of their Halloween, and she laughed. "So he came to school dressed in costume, just because it's Halloween?"

"That's right," Keith agreed.

Mom chuckled. "I thought I liked that fellow from the first time I saw him. Now I know I do." She looked down at her plate, looked back at Keith. "So, why don't you ask Bran to come for dinner tomorrow after play practice? I can cook up some steaks, and then you boys can go to a movie."

Keith stopped, looked into her eyes. "I...I'd like that. Thanks, Mom."

"Well, I was just feeling bad he didn't make it to your physics lab, and I thought maybe you'd like to have a friend over. I miss the way you and Frank used to swap back and forth for meals."

"Thanks, Mom. Thanks a lot."

After dinner Keith found his cast list, with all the phone numbers, and retreated to his room. Three times he picked up the phone before finally forcing himself to dial Bran's number. Then, as one ring followed another, he started to wish that Bran wouldn't answer, that he wouldn't have to go through with asking him over.

"Hello?"

"Uh...hello. May I speak with Bran, please?"

"Who's calling?" The male voice at the other end was gruff; Keith imagined Bran's father as a dark-haired overweight man sitting in his undershirt before the TV, a beer open on the table next to him.

"This is Keith Graff. A friend of Bran's from school."

The phone hit a solid surface with a clunk, and Keith heard some muffled shouting. Then Bran's voice came on, sounding distant. "Keith?"

"Bran?"

"Hi, kid. How're you doing?"

"Oh, fine. How about you? Recovered from today yet?"

Bran chuckled. "Yeah, that was really something. Man, those idiots just can't take a joke, can they? I tell you, when you guys showed up all in costume, I felt like the cavalry was riding over the hill to save John Wayne's ass."

"It was neat."

"So what's up?"

"Mom asked me if I wanted to invite you over here for dinner tomorrow night. Can you come?"

"Dinner? That's awfully nice. You Mom is a great woman. I'm going to nominate her for sainthood, that's what I'm going to do."

"Uh, I think she might be a saint already. But she won't mind. So, can you come to dinner?"

"Sure. Always glad to get some free food. When is this momentous occasion?"

"After play practice."

"Fine."

"And…" Keith took a breath. "She suggested that we might want to go to a movie or something afterwards."

"Ah, she's a regular social secretary, isn't she? What movie were you thinking of?"

Keith named a new science fiction film that he'd been wanting to see.

"That sounds good. Lots of guns and spaceships and shoot-em-up battle scenes." Bran made a few laser noises, and detonated an explosion or two. "Fantastic. Okay, it's a date, then. I'll just come home with you after practice."

"Wonderful."

"Okay, then." There was a lull, and Keith realized with embarrassment that he didn't know how to end the conversation.

"All right," Bran said with enthusiasm. "I'll see you tomorrow then. Good night."

"Good night,' Keith answered automatically, and then he heard a click as Bran hung up.

Good night, he thought, with a warm feeling inside him. And, it's a date.

Good old Mom, he thought, then turned to his homework.

CHAPTER SEVEN

An important event was planned for Friday's rehearsal: the first complete run-through of Act Three. This would be no scene-by-scene casual practice, but a dry run—almost as if it were the night of the play. Keith fidgeted all day. Between the scheduled run-through and dinner with Bran, he had enough on his mind to keep his hands nervously twitching and his thoughts wandering.

Lunch didn't make him feel any less nervous.

All his lunch buddies wore identical t-shirts: blue shirts imprinted with a design of comedy and tragedy masks over the stylized words "Oak Grove." He'd seen them wear the shirts individually before, but this was the first time he'd seen the whole group dressed in them at once. As he and Jane approached the table, Keith felt his stomach churn. *No matter how much I like these people, and they like me…I'm still an outsider. Still a newcomer.*

When they sat down, Bran smiled across the table at Keith. "My boy, I have been chosen —"

"He appointed himself," Laura said.

Bran scowled in her direction, then continued, "Chosen by the assembled multitude to give you a token of our deep feeling for you, and our high regard for your acting talents."

Debbie yawned. "Skip the speech, Bran, and give him the present."

"Present?" Keith asked, sitting up.

"Close your eyes."

He shut his eyes, felt his hands lifted, then felt something placed within them. Cloth.

"Look."

Cautiously, Keith opened his eyes. Cradled in his hands was a shirt identical to the ones the others wore. He looked from face to face, the clasped the shirt to himself with a grin of pure delight. "Thanks!" I'm one of them, he thought. They're telling me that I'm part of the group, that they want me here.

I don't have to be an outsider any more.

"Try it on," Laura said, leaning forward with her chin in her hands.

"Right." Keith slipped the t-shirt over his head, pulling it down to cover his own shirt. It fit a little loosely in the shoulders, but Keith didn't mind—to him it was worth more than a mink coat or a king's robes.

"Gee, I don't know what to say to thank you all."

"Then don't say anything," Debbie said. "You people all want to make speeches. Everything's an occasion for a speech. Bunch of hams, all of you."

Laura smiled sweetly. "You're just sore because you're afraid we'll upstage you."

Debbie stood on her chair, threw her arms out and her head back. "Exactly, my dears. Center stage is where I belong. Now go on with your lunch and leave me to the adoration of my fans."

Bran shook his head. "Sad," he said to no one in particular. "Insanity strikes so suddenly. It's not a pretty sight, is it?"

Keith smiled, his nervousness for the moment forgotten.

*

Rehearsal was mad. Jerry Todd forgot three pages of dialogue, Debbie made two entrances at the wrong times, and Susan Major was in a giggling mood that threatened to engulf the entire cast. But they managed to make it through the third act, and Keith was able to get through his own entrances and speak his lines without incident.

Midway through the act, he exited with Bran and had to stay backstage for a time. As soon as they were out of sight, Keith gave a heavy sigh. "This is terrible. I feel like the play will never work."

Bran looked disapproving. "Stay in character, young man," he said in his best Teddy Roosevelt voice. "If everyone does the same, it'll be just bully."

Mild as the rebuke was, it stung Keith like a nasty bee, and he was quiet the rest of the rehearsal.

When the act was over, Bob Hening gathered the cast together and read some of the notes he'd made on their performances. Then Albert made some more comments, and finally practice was over.

"Hey you guys," Debbie said in the hall, "What say we all go to McDonald's and then do something afterwards?"

"Love to," Bran said. He looked at Keith and smiled. "However, I've been invited as a dinner guest at the Graff household, and I wouldn't think of disappointing the lovely Mrs. Graff."

"Oh," Debbie said, "an exclusive little dinner, eh?"

"Give it a rest, Deb," Laura chimed in. She turned to Keith. "You guys have a good time, okay?"

"Yeah," Debbie said, chuckling. "Anyway, I'm probably going to the movies with Warren tonight. And we can be exclusive too."

Keith shrank back from the hostility in her voice, but Bran just shrugged. "Have it your own way," the older boy said. "I'm looking forward to a good dinner, that's all there is to it." He walked to the door. "Anybody who wants a ride, come on."

Debbie sidled up to Warren and batted her eyelashes. "Want to give me a ride home, big boy?"

Warren slipped an arm around her shoulders. "Fine with me. What movie do you want to see?"

Laura snorted and strode forward to meet Bran. "*I* need a ride."

Albert, carrying his usual large stack of books, joined the two. "Me too."

Keith was unsure what to do. He felt as if some kind of war had suddenly sprung up in the middle of the corridor, and he didn't know why or even who the two sides were. All he knew was that he suddenly felt very uncomfortable, very much in the middle of the front lines.

"Come on, Keith," Bran waved. He caught up with Bran and Laura and Bert, and the four of them left Debbie and Warren behind as they boarded Bran's car. As usual, Keith and Laura sat in the back while Bert took the front seat next to Bran.

As they pulled out of the parking lot, Keith sighed. "What was that all about?"

"Debbie's acting weird again," Bran said. "She does this every so often, when she thinks she isn't getting enough attention. Well, I'm not going to let her ruin a good dinner for me. If she wants to act like a spoiled brat, let her." Bran's tone was a good deal more serious than Keith was used to from his friend.

Laura patted Bran on the shoulder. "It's just an act. Debbie thinks she can get what she wants by acting hurt. It took me a couple of years to find out that if you just ignore her, she'll come out of her snit in a few days." Laura shrugged. "What's it to her if a couple of us want to do things without including her? She's got to learn that she can't be the center of everything."

"Right." Bran grinned. "She can't, because *I'm* the center of everything in this little group. And don't any of you forget it."

"Yes, oh great one," Laura said, feigning a bow.

Keith relaxed. Bran was his old self now, his unaccustomed anger evaporated. He wondered, though, just a little—and worried.

By quarter to six Bran had dropped Bert and Laura off at their homes; on the way to Keith's house he pulled into a neighborhood shopping center and shut off the motor. "What's you mother's favorite color?"

"Huh? Green."

"I'll be right back." Bran left, and ducked into a flower shop. In just a minute or two he reappeared with a bouquet of mixed flowers.

"You didn't have to do that," Keith said, as Bran climbed back into the car.

"I know I didn't. I wanted to. I hope she'll like them."

"Mom loves flowers."

Keith was right—when she saw the flowers, Mom clapped her hands and squealed. "Thank you, Bran." To Keith she said, "Don't suppose you'd want to trade parents with Bran?"

"Not likely," Keith answered with a laugh.

"Come with me," Mom said, leading the way to the kitchen. "I have hot chocolate—I thought it would be just the thing for a cold day like this."

Bran peeled off his jacket and hung it on the coat rack, accepted a cup of cocoa from Keith's mother. The rising steam swirled momentarily around Bran's face, and Keith shivered.

God, he's beautiful.

"So how did practice go?" Mom asked, throwing three good-sized steaks onto the broiler and pausing to stir something on the stove.

"We did all of Act Three," Keith said, "And we managed to get through it alive." He sat at the already-set table, motioned Bran to sit down next to him. "This play may come together yet."

"It'll come together," Bran said, sipping coca. "Wow, that's good. I hadn't realized how cold it is outside." He looked out the kitchen window. "Won't be long before we have snow."

Mom looked up in alarm. "Bite your tongue. Give us a good couple of months of autumn first, please."

Keith leaned back in his chair, a contented smile on this lips and a warm feeling growing in his stomach, helped along by the hot cocoa. Everything was *right*—Bran and Mom were getting along like they were old friends. Keith remembered how his friend Frank had been almost part of the family—Frank knew his way around the Graff house as well as he knew his own, and often he stopped by for a snack or just to say hello when Keith wasn't even home.

That's what I want for Bran, Keith thought. I want him to be part of my life.

The click of a fork brought Keith back to reality with a jar, and he was suddenly abashed at the direction his thoughts were taking. Jeez, it's like I've got the two of us married already. Stop it, Keith boy, or you'll be setting yourself up for the biggest disappointment you've ever suffered—worse than finding out just how boring it was to be able to stay up and watch adult shows on TV.

Over dinner, his mother kept conversation going, encouraging Bran to talk without seeming to pry into his life. Finally the talk turned to classes and Mom asked, "What kind of work are you thinking of going into, Bran? Or have you decided yet?"

"Umm." Bran swallowed his mouthful, looked up with his fork balanced in his hand. "I'm going to be a professional actor."

"Have you decided what school you're going to? Or are you going to run away to New York to seek your fortune?" Her tone told both boys just what she thought of *that* idea.

"No," Bran said. "I've applied to a couple of schools...I'm hoping to get into Patapsco University, in Maryland. They have a good drama program...Debbie's sister goes there."

"Not one of the big acting colleges? You're not going to try for a spot on Broadway?"

Bran shook his head. "I'm not trying to be a superstar, I just want to act. Dinner theaters, regional touring companies ...anything. Just so I get to be on stage."

Mom nodded. "Well, I wish you luck. At least you know what you want—not many people your age can say that."

After dinner Keith's mother refused to let the two boys help clear the table. "Go on," she said, "Don't be late for your movie. I'll take care of the dishes." At the door, she gave Keith a kiss and squeezed Bran's hand. "Don't be a stranger, Bran. You're welcome any time you want to come."

"Thanks for a great dinner, Mrs. Graff. I'm sure I'll see you again sometime soon."

During the movie Keith found it hard to keep his eyes on the screen. His gaze kept wandering to Bran's face, half-lit in the darkened theater, eyes intent on the movie. Keith kept his hands in his lap, and was careful to avoid brushing Bran's arm too much with his own.

I don't want him to think I'm trying to make a move on him, Keith thought. I don't want him uncomfortable. Just let it be like it was at dinner, calm and friendly, without any pressure. That's all I ask.

When the movie was over Bran insisted on going out for ice cream, then decided it would be cheaper to get one large hot fudge sundae that they could split. Keith agreed, and soon they were both laughing and having spoon-fights in the middle of the ice cream.

It was well past eleven when Keith got home; Bran pulled up in front of the house and stopped the car, but kept the engine running.

Keith took a breath, ready to ask Bran in…then he forced himself to stop. It had been a wonderful night; he didn't dare ruin it by being too forward. And he didn't trust himself too far. Besides, if Bran had wanted to come in he could have shut off the car.

"Good night," Keith said, hopping out of the car.

"Hey," Bran said, leaning across the seat, "thanks a lot. I really had a good time. Thank your mother for me too, you hear?"

"I will."

"Okay. Bye."

The car drove away, and Keith gave a halfhearted little wave. The night was chilly, and he shivered under his windbreaker. It was getting time to take out the winter coats.

Still shivering, he sat down on the front steps and looked toward the sky. There were only a few clouds low in the east, and the moon was nowhere to be seen; the stars were unusually bright. Keith picked out a few of the easiest constellations, then simply sat with his eyes skyward, losing himself in the starry night.

After a while, a shooting star dashed by. Keith realized he was freezing from sitting on the cold steps, and he roused himself. Mom was asleep; he let himself into the house and grabbed a quick glass of milk before going up to his room. A few pages of reading was enough to put him in a drowsy mood; he turned off the light and curled up under his covers. Sleep came quickly.

*

The phone woke Keith. Sunlight was streaming in his windows; he glanced at the clock and saw that it was half past nine.

"Hello?"

"Keith? Hi, how are you?"

It took him a second to place the voice, then he sat up excitedly in bed. "Frank?"

"Yep. How are you doing, fella?"

"Fine. Hey, it's good to hear from you."

"Yeah, well, there's a story behind that."

"Are you calling from home?" Keith imagined Frank sitting in his own living room, talking on his mother's absurd Mickey Mouse phone.

"No, I'm not, actually."

"Where are you?"

"Well, right now we're at a truck stop about two hundred miles from you."

"Where?"

"Dad had to make a business trip out to your neck of the woods. I badgered him until he said he'd bring me along. We were on a plane yesterday and then we went around to different offices; Dad's got more places to visit today."

"When will you be here?" Keith wanted to jump for joy. He hadn't seen Frank for months.

"Four hours, maybe? Dad has to be back tomorrow night; can I stay at your place tonight? It'll be good to see you again."

"Sure." Keith jumped out of bed and pulled on his robe. "Hey, Frank, let me check things with Mom just to make sure. Can you hold on?"

"Okay."

His mother was watching TV over breakfast, and was delighted to hear of Frank's sudden visit. "Of course he can stay over. Ask him if his Dad will drop him here, or does he want us to come get him somewhere?"

Keith got back on the phone and conferred with Frank. "Our house is right on the way for his Dad—how about if you get on and give him directions?"

"All right." She took the phone. "Mark? Alice here. We're a good ways off the Interstate, are you sure you don't want me to meet you somewhere?" She listened for a moment. "Okay, I guess you're right. Do you have a piece of paper? Once you get in the state, you want exit twelve…."

Keith ran upstairs and started to clean his room by throwing things under the bed and in dresser drawers. Frank! He had been feeling guilty about not talking to Frank…it would be great to have his friend here. And for a whole day. And….

He suddenly froze, standing in the middle of his room with a shirt in one hand and a pair of jeans in the other.

Frank.

I've been thinking so much about Bran lately, I've nearly forgotten Frank?

How could he have forgotten? His first weeks in Oak Grove, all he did was miss Frank. Now his erstwhile dreams were coming true, Frank was visiting, and he only had eyes for another boy.

It was going to be an interesting visit.

CHAPTER EIGHT

Frank had grown. That was the first thing Keith noticed when his friend hopped out of the big rental car that pulled up in front of Keith's house. Frank used to be shorter than me, Keith thought, and in just a few months he's matched my height.

"Keith!"

"Frank!" Keith flew down the front steps and threw his arms around Frank. For a long minute the boys hugged each other as tightly as they could, then Keith drew back and waved to Frank's father. "Hi, Mr. Mark. Come on in, my mom is anxious to see you." Turning back to Frank, he said, "How long can you stay? Where's your luggage? How's school? What play are you doing?"

"Slow down." Frank handed him a bulging overnight bag. "Let's get inside and you can show me around, then we'll have plenty of time to get caught up."

"Right. Follow me."

Over the next hour or so, as Keith showed Frank around and got all the news of the old neighborhood, he watched Frank almost shyly. Blond and gangly, Frank had been Keith's friend since the two of them were in fourth grade. In the year or so before Keith moved, his friendship with Frank had developed in directions that were a little scary, if intensely exciting. Now...well, he wanted to just pick up with Frank as if things were the same, but he wasn't sure he could.

Have I changed *that* much, in these few months?

They wound up in Keith's room; Keith flopped down on his bed while Frank stood at the window, looking out. "This is a nice house," Frank said. "Are you getting used to it?"

"I hated it the first week or so." Keith looked around himself. "But yeah, I'm getting used to it. Still, I don't think I'll ever forget the old house. Who's living there now?"

"An old man and lady. They're retired or something. They have poodles...three of them. They're putting up a fence around the back yard."

Keith shook his head. "Guess there won't be any tree-climbing now." Keith's back yard had the only tree in the neighborhood that was worth climbing, an old oak with three great limbs and a thousand branches. "So tell me about your trip."

Frank leaned against the desk, folded his arms across him chest. "It was neat. We took a plane yesterday afternoon, and picked up a rental car at the airport. Last night Dad met with one of his representatives, and then we stayed in a hotel." He dimpled. "It'll be better staying here tonight. I just wish we weren't going back so soon." His clear blue eyes met Keith's. "I've missed you, guy."

The phone rang, and Keith looked away apologetically. "Hold on, let me get that." He picked it up. "Hello?"

"Hi, kid."

"Bran. What's up?"

"We're getting together a touch football game over at the church near Laura's house. Want to play?"

"Uh...when?"

"Five o'clock. Jane's going to bring her guitar—"

"Does it play football?"

"For singing afterwards, nitwit. At Laura's."

"Hold on." Keith covered the mouthpiece, looked at Frank. "Want to play touch football tonight with a bunch of friends of mine?"

"Sure."

"Here, hold the phone. I have to ask Mom."

Keith ran downstairs and explained the plans. "Can we go?"

"Of course. Why don't you take the car? Then you and Frank can stay out as late as you want."

"Really? Gee, thanks, Mom. You're the greatest."

"Can I have that in writing?"

Keith picked up the kitchen phone and was surprised to hear Bran talking. "I'm back," he interrupted.

Frank's voice answered him. "I was just talking to your friend Bran. This sounds like a crazy group."

"It is. Hey, Bran, we can go. We'll meet you there at five, okay?"

"You don't need a ride?"

"Mom's letting me use the car."

"Big time, eh?" Bran said. "Good. I'll see you there. I'm looking forward to meeting you, Frank. Bye, kids." He hung up.

Frank met Keith halfway down the stairs. "Okay," he said, "I'm impressed. You've been gone since July, and already you have friends." He grinned. "I'll bet you don't miss Kinwood at all."

"Of course I do." Keith went back to his room and sat down on the bed. Frank sat next to him. "I'll always miss you and the neighborhood. I was miserable until last month. Then I got involved in the play, and all these crazy drama people, and…well, things are a lot better, that's all."

"I was worried about you. Your last couple letters sounded depressed, and then you stopped writing."

"I got busy."

"I know."

Keith was suddenly very conscious of Frank's nearness, of Frank's body pressed against his right side. Very aware of Frank's concern. All at once he was so filled with love for Frank that he felt he could scream. *He cares about me and I care about him, and however things are going here I've missed him more than I want to admit.*

A second later, Keith turned and Frank quite naturally put his arms around him. An instant after that, the two boys clung to one another, hugging tightly and pressing their faces together.

"I miss you so much," Frank said. "And...and seeing you here, I just realize that it's permanent, you're really gone."

"I've missed you too."

"Keith." Frank stroked his hair, just as he'd done a thousand times in the year before. Frank's lips met his, and as they kissed. Frank tightened his arms around Keith, held him more securely. Keith in turn pulled Frank even closer, then closed his eyes and gently pulled away.

"I...I can't."

"What's wrong?" Frank said, his face lined with concern, his hands still lingering comfortingly on Keith's shoulders.

"It's not fair to you. I j-just caught myself...wishing it was...someone else." Ashamed, Keith looked down.

Frank lifted Keith's chin, looked into his eyes. "I'm sorry, boy. I didn't know. Who is it?"

"You just talked to him on the phone. Bran."

Frank nodded knowingly. "And does he love you?"

"I...I don't know." Keith felt very close to crying.

"Tell me about it."

As Frank listened patiently, Keith told him the story of the past month.

*

The football game, an impromptu Saturday afternoon get-together, involved most of the cast of the play. Keith and Frank teamed up with Bran, Bert, Warren, and Debbie; they played against Jane and Laura helped out by Jerry Todd, Jane's friend Rick Lederman, and Dale Sullivan and Mark Greenberg. Dale and Mark had minor roles in the play; beyond that, they kept to themselves most of the time.

It was hard to tell which team actually won. They scrambled around a lot on the football field adjacent to Laura's small church, chasing Warren's half-deflated football and shouting quite a bit. When it started to rain Bran announced loudly that his team had won by a score of seventeen to nothing, and that seemed to end the game.

During the two-block run to Laura's house, Laura tried to argue the closing score.

"It was seventeen to nothing, our favor," Bran stubbornly insisted.

Laura threw up her arms in mock exasperation. "It's *always* seventeen to nothing in your favor. No matter what team you're on."

"I'm always scorekeeper."

Laura glanced at Frank, the obvious newest face. "The only time it's smart to be on the team opposing Bran is when we play miniature golf."

Laura herded everyone into her cozy basement, then vanished to return a few minutes later with mugs of cocoa and a handful of towels.

Frank and Keith shared a towel. Frank nodded in Bran's direction. "That's him."

"Uh-huh. What do you think?"

"Not sure yet. But I suspect that you have good taste."

In no time Jane was convinced to bring out her guitar, and everyone settled into chairs or on the floor to listen and sing along. The mood was light and friendly, and Keith was glad Frank was able to see everyone like this.

After a while Jane handed her guitar over to Laura, who carefully strummed out a few tunes. Jane herself curled up next to Rick Lederman, who put his arm around her. Keith had already noticed Dale Sullivan and Mark Greenberg holding hands. He gave Frank a tender smile, but didn't move toward his friend. Frank seemed to understand.

"I'm tired," Laura said, holding up the guitar. When there were no takers, she turned on the radio instead. The conversation drifted past Keith and Frank—the latest scandal about the cheerleaders, complaints about the advanced algebra test, discussions of the relative merits of all the latest movies.

Then, abruptly, Keith found himself involved in a complicated and mysterious exchange. He was looking at Bran, thinking nothing in particular but sort of half-daydreaming, when he suddenly became aware of the direction of other eyes. Debbie, for example, also had her gaze fixed on Bran. Bran was looking at Warren. Warren was gazing off into space at nothing in particular.

Bran turned, saw that Keith was looking at him, and moved his eyes across the room hastily. Then Keith felt eyes on him, and he turned to see Debbie glaring straight at him. On her face was the tail-end of a look of anger, just in the process of being replaced by a satisfied half-smile.

She knows, Keith thought. She knows that I'm in love with Bran.

He didn't know how he knew…but his knowledge was absolute. Her face had revealed the contents of her mind, and she knew.

And Bran….

Bran was staring at Warren, and when I caught him at it he looked away, as if he were embarrassed.

Might Debbie be right about Bran and Warren?

As if to destroy his speculation, Bran met Debbie's eyes, smiled, and beckoned her over to him. She leaned her head on his shoulder, and he absently stroked her hair, looking contented.

Debbie looked back at Keith, and he could swear that her eyes flashed with malice. I have him, she seemed to say, and you can't.

Frank touched Keith on the arm, and the spell was broken. "Do you think we ought to be getting home?"

Keith looked at his watch—it was pushing nine-thirty. "Oh, sure. You were up early this morning, weren't you?"

"And on the road a lot," Frank agreed. Keith read the unspoken message underneath Frank's words: *I've seen enough, friend, and I think we should talk.*

Keith made goodbyes, and the two boys dashed to the car through driving rain.

"So what do you think?" Keith asked when they were safely in the car.

Frank stared off into the wet night. "Wait 'til we get home. I'm still pondering."

At home they took a plate of cookies and a jug of milk upstairs, then sat together on Keith's bed with the lights off, watching the rain.

"Okay," Frank said, "You've got good taste. I like him. Is he always so...crazy?"

"Not all the time. I've seen him when he's awfully serious. Usually about acting. I...I think the craziness is one of his acts, to keep himself defended. I don't think he's comfortable about letting people too close."

"Hmm," Frank said, "That doesn't make it any too easy to figure out what he's thinking. I guess your problem is, you don't know what he wants from you."

"More like whether he wants what I do. I don't think he does."

"Maybe not." Frank took the time to demolish a cookie. "He looked pretty serious with that girl...Debbie?"

"Yeah."

"But you never know. He's a friendly guy, and some people just take advantage of that. And Debbie looks like the kind of person who would take advantage."

"Did you see what went on just before we left?"

"You mean when you were daydreaming about him, and Debbie was looking daggers at you?"

"Is that how you interpreted it?"

"Uh-huh. She knows how you feel about him, even if *he* doesn't. And whatever the situation is between them, she considers him her property and she doesn't like you trying to muscle in."

Keith looked miserable. "I'm not trying to muscle in. If Bran wants Debbie, I'm not going to do anything to make him uncomfortable. I…I just want to know for *sure*."

Frank put out an arm, and Keith moved into his friend's embrace.

"I'll tell you something else," Frank said. "And one reason I'm not at all sure about your friend Bran. For a minute there, it almost seemed that he was looking at Warren the same way you were looking at *him*."

Keith nodded, feeling even more wretched. "That's one theory. That Bran and Warren are…" he couldn't finish.

"And how do you feel about that?"

Keith swallowed. "Same as with Debbie. If Bran's happy, I don't want to come between him and anybody."

"Poor kid. What are you going to do?"

"I don't know. Just sit around a let things go on as they have been, I guess. Sooner or later Bran's going to do something that will make me sure one way or another. Then…I guess I'll do my best to forget about him. Romantically, I mean —I still want to be his friend."

"He's a lucky guy." Frank squeezed Keith comfortingly. "I'm worried about you, fella. You're not having a great time with all this. Maybe you should stop torturing yourself."

"How?"

"Tell him how you feel."

"Right." Keith frowned. "Then he gets all uptight, and starts cooling the friendship, and then pretty soon I don't see him any more."

"Then give up on him. Start hanging around with some other people. There's got to be other groups you could spend time with."

"But…."

"But?" Frank said, looking right into Keith's eyes.

"But then I wouldn't be able to see him at all," Keith said, surprising himself.

"You poor kid. You've really fallen, haven't you?"

"I...I guess so."

"Then there's just one way for it to work out," Frank said, as if he had just settled the whole matter.

"How?"

"He's just going to have to fall in love with you. That's all there is to it."

"Thanks."

"I'm sorry. So let's change the subject. Tell me about you classes. Are you keeping up with German?"

"I'm in German Three." Keith was a little grateful that Frank allowed the topic of Bran to drop. He and Frank spent the next hour comparing classes, and then he encouraged Frank to talk about the old neighborhood.

Frank had pictures in his bag, and he brought them out to show Keith—kids from the old place, Frank and his family, even a few shots of Keith's old house. He had to admit that he didn't care for what the new owners had done to the place.

Eventually both Frank and Keith were yawning and stretching, and Keith found it hard to keep his eyes open. Frank looked at him apologetically.

"I guess it's time to start thinking about going to sleep." Frank lifted his bag, started to the door. "If you'll show me where you keep spare sheets and blankets, I can get the couch ready."

Keith frowned. "You've never slept on the couch before."

"I just thought...."

"Frank, you're about the best buddy a guy could possibly have. Forget sleeping on the couch. You stay with me, the way we always do."

Frank shrugged. "Whatever you say. Hey, Keith, you don't have to worry, I'm not going to...."

Keith held up a hand to silence the older boy. "Fella, I'm never going to worry about sleeping with you. Do you want the bathroom first?"

"I guess so."

A few minutes later Frank returned, wearing green pajamas. Keith visited the bathroom himself; when he came back he found Frank sitting on the bed.

"So, which side do you want?"

Keith shrugged. "I don't care." He shivered. "I'm cold."

Frank threw back the covers, opened his arms. "Get in here, then."

With Frank's arms folded warmly around him, and the covers tucked up under his chin, Keith felt much more secure. He turned his head and looked into Frank's eyes. "I didn't mean for you to spend your whole time here taking care of me. It's rotten of me to be complaining all the time like this. Thanks for being so patient."

"Just hush. I think of it as insurance. Sometime in the next few years I'm probably going to have to spend some time complaining to you, and I want to know that you'll be there to take care of me." Frank chuckled, and Keith joined the laughter...but he knew that there was a thread of seriousness under his friend's words.

"I'm sorry, Frank. Don't worry, you'll have your chance too. I just hope I'll be as good to you as you've been to me."

"Just shut up and stop apologizing." Frank put his finger to Keith's lips, then moved his face close and gave Keith a quick kiss. "Go to sleep, fella. I'll take care of you."

Keith turned his back toward Frank, pressed his body against his friend, and pulled Frank's arms tight across his chest. Protected and happy, he drifted off to sleep.

Keith woke chilly and disoriented in the middle of the night. His dreams had been confused, all about Frank and Bran and an endless football game that never seemed to reach first down. He was laying on his back; at his side he heard Frank's steady soft breathing. His room was quiet, not even the rush of wind outside or the dripping of rain from the roof.

He turned on his side, faced Frank, and for a while he lay still, floating in and out of sleep and wakefulness. Then he became conscious of the fact that his right arm draped over Frank's body felt good where it was.

Frank stirred, and Keith moved closer. It was almost unnaturally dark; only the distant pale light of a streetlamp shone through the windows, and it gave only enough light to make out forms and layer upon layer of shadows. Feeling as if he moved in a dream, Keith stroked Frank's hair, then bent over his sleeping friend and placed a kiss on his forehead.

This is what it's supposed to be like, Keith thought.

They were both fully awake now. Frank hugged Keith, rubbed his back through the thin material of his pajama tops. Keith slipped one hand under Frank's shirt and massaged his chest. Warm, Frank was so warm. And solid.

"Wait," Frank whispered.

In response, Keith kissed him again.

After a time, Frank said, "I'm sorry."

"What for?"

"That I'm not Bran."

Keith silenced him with a firm embrace. "You're Frank. That's what I want." Deliberately, he kissed Frank, then moved his hands down along Frank's body, questing.

We've gone this far before, Keith thought. But no further. Now I *know* that I want to, I know that I love Frank. And isn't this just a way of expressing love?

He had time for one last insane thought—Bran wouldn't mind—and then he was much too busy to think.

CHAPTER NINE

The boys slept late Sunday morning; it was close to ten-thirty when Keith finally struggled awake. In the morning light Frank's face was happily peaceful, the outline of a smile traced around his relaxed mouth. Automatically Keith bent toward him, then stopped.

I love you, Frank. You've given me what I needed...but I don't think either of us is ready to start behaving like lovestruck schoolgirls. You'll always be my friend, always be welcome in my life. Let's not ruin that friendship.

Keith hopped out of bed, found his pajamas in the tangle of clothes on the floor, and visited the bathroom. When he returned, Frank was sitting up.

There was a sparkle in Frank's eyes, and he wore a broad grin. "Good morning. What's for breakfast?"

"I'll see what we can dig up. Mom's probably awake, maybe I can con her into making something." Silently, Keith gave thanks that Frank didn't say anything about last night.

After breakfast the two boys watched a little television, and then Keith took Frank for a walk around the neighborhood. The trees had dropped almost all their leaves, and the air was distinctly chilly now even when the sun was out.

They didn't talk much. That was one thing Keith had always liked about himself and Frank—they were good enough friends that they didn't *have* to talk all the time, on some occasions they could be silent with one another. Gestures, sideways glances, and accidental touches here and there told the whole story: Frank agreed with Keith. They should not threaten their friendship by getting too involved with other things.

The rest of the day passed calmly. Frank's father drove up shortly after dark, and took Keith's mother and the two boys out to dinner. By eight o'clock Frank was gone, and all Keith had left was memory, and the lingering warmth of the goodbye kiss they'd snuck in out of the grownups' sight.

Silently, Keith finished up his homework, and then went to bed early. As he had been doing lately, he took Bran's shirt to bed with him, and fell asleep feeling cold and lonely once again.

*

With only two weeks to go before the play, activity shifted into high gear at school. Keith volunteered to help with set construction, so any time he wasn't actually rehearsing he worked with Bran and members of the stage crew in the back of the auditorium. The work was easy—hammering, painting, moving unwieldy wood-and-canvas flats into place on stage.

Tuesday afternoon Bob Hening concentrated on the major actors, so Keith got a chance to work closely with Bran for a few hours. They took huge flats into the cafeteria, laid them out on the floor, and started painting.

"Think of it as painting your living room," Bran said, "Only stretched out on the floor."

Keith smiled. "I did enough room painting when we moved in…this is much easier."

After twenty minutes or so, Keith looked up. "Bran?"

"Yeah?"

"Do you remember your mother?"

Bran put down his paintbrush, cocked his head and stared at Keith. "What kind of question is that?"

Keith shrugged. "I don't know. Sometimes…well, I used to get mad at my father, because he and Mom got divorced. And

I always wanted to talk to somebody about it, but I never felt right. Finally I said something to Frank, and I felt a lot better." He sighed. "It occurred to me that you never talk about your mother." He shook his head. "Never mind."

"No, don't be sorry." Bran picked up his brush and started spreading paint with wide strokes. After a moment of silence he said, "Yeah, I miss her. We used to have a lot of fun, the whole family. Dad changed a lot when Mother died." He was silent a while longer, then he looked at Keith again. "And it's like you said. I guess I'm still mad at her, a little, because she left us. Isn't *that* an awful thing to say?"

"No." Keith put down his own brush and moved in Bran's direction. The boys were both on their knees; Keith tousled Bran's hair gently, afraid that the older boy would draw back. "If that's the way you feel, what can you do about it? It's natural to feel mad at her."

"I've never talked to anybody about Mother."

"Nobody?" Keith whistled. At least when Dad left, he had Frank to talk to.

"Not even Dad. Oh, my brother tried to get me to talk about it, but that was right after she...anyway, I didn't feel like saying anything." He looked into Keith's eyes. "That was two years ago. It doesn't seem that long."

"Did you cry?"

"Boy, you're just filled with these questions today, aren't you? Of course I cried. What do you mean asking a fool question like that?"

"Just thinking how I'd feel if my mother died. Wow, I think I'd cry nonstop for a week. And you're right, I'd be really angry at her."

"It's no picnic. But hey, life goes on, right? You picked up after your father left. Me and my dad, we kept going without Mother."

"D-did your father cry?"

Bran looked up, startled. "If he did, I never saw him."

They were quiet for a while longer, then Keith said, "Well, look, if you ever want to talk about it..."

Bran nodded. "Thanks, kid." He looked puzzled. "You know, you're the only one of my friends who's ever asked about Mother, just like that."

"Maybe everybody thinks they shouldn't talk about it." Keith went back to his painting. "Like when my dog died, back when I was ten. Nobody would say anything—I guess they were all afraid I'd crack up or something. Mom and Dad threw out all her toys. Everybody kept on not mentioning Fluffy, as if she were still alive." He chuckled. "Damn it, I knew she wasn't still alive. I just wanted people to admit it and get on with things."

Again Bran tilted his head. "Kid, you're a lot smarter than you look."

"Thanks. I guess."

"I'll have to keep an eye on you. I have this strange feeling that you have everybody all figured out—you know just what makes us all tick."

Keith couldn't help laughing. "I can't even figure *myself* out."

"We'll see." Bran went on painting, then muttered once more, "We'll see."

*

Whenever Keith was with Bran, he was happy. He began to be affected by Bran's crazy mannerisms, and the two of them took to doing unplanned little dramatic scenes at lunch time.

"Aha, Smithers," Bran cried when Keith approached, "So you've returned to the scene of the crime, to gloat over your victims, no doubt."

"Yes, Inspector Johnson, I've returned. Returned to see that you never carry the tale of my deeds to the authorities." Keith whipped out an imaginary gun, and pumped Bran full of bullets. Bran collapsed on the floor and spend a full five minutes dying.

The next day, Bran slammed down his plastic fork and stared at his cafeteria tray. "Doctor," he gasped, "I think...I think some of our experimental culture may have taken over the kitchens. I-I don't know if I can go on. It feels as if I'm... changing." Bran bared his teeth and snarled.

"Get a grip on yourself, Reginald," Keith said, jumping up in mock alarm. "We can easily reverse the polarity of the neutron flow. Reginald...put down that test tube. Reginald... aargh!" Now it was Keith's turn to die, and he did it with much choking and twitching. When he lay still on the floor, Debbie stepped over him. "I'm going to get some french fries. Anyone else want some?"

When Keith wasn't in Bran's company, he found himself brooding more often than not. He sat through his classes quietly, paying attention to the teacher but not keeping his mind fully on his work; at home he watched TV or read paperback mysteries from the library, and did his best not to think of Bran. And at night, he curled up in his bed and had trouble getting to sleep.

Friday night, a week before the play, Keith was watching a movie on TV with his mother. Neither of them paid much attention—she leafed through magazines while Keith stared off into space, lost in the plot of an Agatha Christie book. During a commercial, his mother put down her magazine and looked across the room at Keith.

"Son, is there anything bothering you?"

"Huh? No, nothing's wrong."

"You've been morose lately. Aren't things going well in school?"

Keith shrugged. "Okay, I guess."

"Is it the play, then? Are rehearsals going okay?"

"Fine."

"I'm not trying to pry. I'm just worried about you. Is it Frank? Is everything okay between the two of you?"

Keith blushed. "Everything's okay."

Mom nodded, then she looked off into the distance. "I remember when I was in high school. I was madly in love with Danny Tripler, the captain of the basketball team. Of course, he didn't even know I was alive. And my mother kept badgering me with the same kind of questions I'm badgering you with." She returned her gaze to him. "I'm sorry, Keith. I never thought I'd hear myself doing that to *my* child."

Her look of concern was so strong, Keith's heart melted. Damn it, if he couldn't talk to his own mother....

"You know my friend Bran," he said, trying to sound off-handed.

"Yes."

"Well...I guess he's like Danny Tripler."

She took a breath, then let out a long sigh. Keith felt his stomach twist into a knot.

"Mom?"

She gave him a reassuring smile. "Don't worry, son. I...I guess I expected this, but I didn't go so far as to figure out what I was going to say." She considered her hands for a moment. "So you're...gay?"

"I never really thought of it that way. But I guess I am."

"I wondered about you and Frank, now and again. It wasn't any of my business, of course, but you know how mothers are."

Keith forced a nod. "Frank and I never really...until he was up here..." He was so confused—he didn't know what he ought to be saying. "Are you...mad?"

"Mad?" His mother looked surprised. "Why should I be mad? Good heavens, son, you don't think that I love you any less? Of course not. I don't care who you're attracted to—you're still the same boy you've always been."

Keith swallowed, no trusting himself to speak.

She looked at him, her face open and caring. "I'm just glad that you can finally share this with me. As long as *you* don't have any problems, I certainly don't."

"I don't have any problem with being attracted to boys. It's the *particular* boy who's my major problem right now."

Mom nodded. "Do you want to tell me about it?"

"Not much to tell. I...Mom, I don't know how he feels about me."

"Have you asked him?"

"No." Keith struggled to find the words to express his confused emotions. Mom waited patiently. "If he doesn't feel the same way I do, then...well, it would change the way he looks at me. He might not want anything to do with me again. Or he might be careful about being alone with me, that sort of thing." Keith sighed. "Or, worse, he might feel sorry for me. I don't think I could take that."

Mom nodded sympathy and agreement. "You know best. But suppose he *does* feel the same way?"

"Then it'll work out one way or another."

"Are you sure? Suppose Bran is thinking the same things you're thinking, and he doesn't want to let you know for fear of hurting your friendship? Then you might never know."

Keith looked at his mother with agonized indecision. "It's too much to chance."

"It's your life to run as you see fit, son. But can I give you a word of advice?"

"Of course."

"Sometimes you have to take chances in life, if you're going to be happy. You have to be willing to be hurt, in order to gain anything. Sometimes, even, getting hurt makes you stronger. So that next time, you'll be able to risk more."

"Dad hurt you."

"And I've survived. I'm happy. Without your father, I would never have *you*. I wouldn't have my job. Life is a trade-off, son, between risks and benefits."

"Like life insurance."

She smiled. "Like that, yes. If what you want is important enough, then you're willing to take more risks for it."

"I guess you're right. I'll...I'll have to think about how much I want to risk."

"Keith...I just want you to know that I'm proud of you. You're doing a good job of adjusting to the new place. I know you miss Kinwood, but you haven't tried to make me feel guilty for taking you away from there. I appreciate it. I want you to be happy. If I can do anything, please tell me."

"Thanks, Mom." Keith got up and hugged her, shaking with emotion. "I think I'll go upstairs now. I have to do some thinking."

"Good night, son."

*

Saturday night there was another gathering at Debbie's house, an emergency study session for a surprise algebra test Monday. Even though Keith wasn't in the same math class as the rest, he went to Debbie's, and spent most of his time tending the stereo and making words by biting pretzels into the shape of letters.

Bran stayed with Debbie the whole night, his arm around her most of the time.

That night, Keith felt closer than ever to crying himself to sleep. Instead, he lost himself in a mystery novel, and only turned off the lights when he couldn't keep his eyes open another paragraph.

By Monday morning he felt a lot better. It was the last week of rehearsals and the play was coming together beautifully. Even Jerry Todd was doing well. Growing anticipation over opening night blocked out everything else in his life, and the week passed so quickly that he could hardly believe that Friday night wasn't really Wednesday afternoon.

"Break a leg!" Mom called out to him when Bran showed up to pick him up shortly after six.

"You'll be there?" Keith said, worriedly.

"I'll be there. Go, and do a good job."

"Bye." He kissed her, then dashed out to the car.

The whole gang was strangely silent before the performance. Keith struggled against rising nervousness, then finally gave in to an attack of stage fright when he was alone on the lighting deck. He sat in a corner, hugged himself, and trembled.

After a few minutes of this he felt ready to face the world and went to get into his costume and put on his makeup.

At long last the auditorium was filling, and the cast stood backstage together, waiting out the last ten minutes before they went on.

Laura grinned weakly at Keith. Then she looked around the faces lit only by low red stage lights. "Group hug," she whispered. Keith smiled, and joined the rest in a circle of bodies all pressed together for mutual reassurance.

Then the play started.

Later, Keith didn't remember much of the play. Most of the time he sat backstage, ready to jump when he was needed to retrieve a prop or fetch last-minute articles from the stage crew room. When he went on in the middle of the third act, he was completely the aged and tottering Mr. Witherspoon—for the duration, Keith Graff was utterly submerged.

Only after the curtain call did Keith's tension break, when Bran threw his arms around him and lifted him a clear foot off the stage. "Whoopee!" Bran cried, then put Keith down and hugged an unsuspecting Bert.

Jubilation reined. Fellow students came backstage to congratulate the actors, parents appeared, and in the midst of all the excitement Keith found himself bundled into Bran's back seat and driven to Debbie's house for the cast party.

The party was held in Debbie's large basement. There were food and sodas, and a large ice chest with chilled cans of beer. Keith declined the beer, but he saw that quite a few of the others, Warren and Bran in particular, were drinking the stuff rather heavily.

"Don't worry about them," Laura said, gesturing for Keith to sit next to her on the stairs. "Debbie's parents won't let anybody drive home if they've been drinking. They can either stay here, or Mr. Richard will drive them to where they belong. We've had cast parties here before."

"That's good." He looked at Bran, who was gleefully tossing M&Ms into the air and trying to catch them in his mouth. He succeeded about half the time.

"You don't drink?" Laura asked.

"No. Never tried it."

"Good." She shivered. "It scares me. I wish they wouldn't do it so much. But what the hell, it's not every day we have a cast party, right?"

Keith couldn't help hearing the melancholy tone in her voice. "What's wrong? Don't you think the play went well?"

Laura turned away. "Nothing. Yes, it was a great play."

Now Keith was really concerned. It wasn't like Laura to dismiss an opportunity to talk. "Hey, tell me. Can I help?"

"Oh, Keith." She looked close to tears. "Okay, but you've got to promise not to breathe a word of this."

"I promise. What's bothering you?"

She sighed. "It's love, I'm afraid. I thought I was immune. Sadly, not true."

"Love?" Keith said, stupidly. "Who...?"

Laura nodded toward Bran. "Our good Mr. Davenport there. Oh, I know, I don't have a chance. I could never compete with Debbie. She's better-looking than I am, she's a better actor, she's even better in math."

Keith shook his head. It seemed that everyone was in love with Bran. Debbie, and himself...now Laura.

Why did life have to be so complicated?

Laura patted his hand. "So you see, Keith, there's my problem. Don't fret about me, I'll get over it quickly enough. Run along and have a good time. Don't let me stop you with my woes."

"Don't be stupid." Keith took a deep breath but found that he couldn't tell her about his own feelings for Bran. She would think he was just trying to play for sympathy. "I know how it feels. I…was in love with somebody who wasn't in love with me."

"What did you do?"

"Lived with it," he lied. "And I found out that I could be just friends with this person, that all the romance faded away after a while." Was he lying? In a way, wasn't that what had happened with him and Frank? "Lovers are easy enough to find…we've got all our lives to do that. But it's harder to find good friends. I just decided that friendship was too important to risk with all this love nonsense." He almost believed what he was saying.

After talking to Mom, he thought, *I was almost ready to tell Bran. But now…well, why* can't *I learn to be his friend without wanting more?*

"You're a lot stronger than I am," Laura said.

"How long has it been going on?"

"What, Bran? I guess I've been in love with him since I first met him. But it didn't get bad until a few weeks ago. I've been brooding too much."

"Yeah, I can see how that could happen."

Another sigh. "Like you say, Keith, it'll pass. I just have to learn to live with it for now." She forced a smile. "Thanks an awful lot. It's good to know there's someone I can talk to. You promise you won't tell anyone?"

"I promise, already."

"I'd just die if Debbie found out. I know what she'd do, she'd go out of her way to make sure I saw the two of them together. Debbie can be kind of cruel when she wants to."

"Don't panic. She won't learn from me."

"I hope you don't mind," Laura said, "that I've been hanging around you so much. You're a good guy to talk to, fun to be with…I guess you take my mind off him. And it throws Debbie off the track."

"I guess I don't mind."

For a while they were quiet, forgotten as the party swirled around them. Laura suddenly said, "What about you and the other person? Are you still friends?"

"We still see one another," Keith said, trying to sound wise and soothing while making an effort to be convincing as well. "Of course, moving from the old neighborhood didn't help. But yeah, I'd have to say that things are working out pretty good now."

There was another moment of silence, while Bran and Debbie cleared away furniture and started dancing together. They were joined by Jane and Rick Lederman.

Laura cupped her chin in her hands. "I just wish he wouldn't get so involved with Debbie. I don't want to say bad things about her, but I don't think she's good for Bran. You know, she's interested in Warren also. And I know she'd steal Rick away in a second if Jane ever showed signs of letting him go." She shrugged. "I don't know, I think Bran deserves better. If not me, I'd like to see him with someone who would treat him better."

"You don't think Debbie's going to hurt him bad, do you?" Keith asked, suddenly concerned in a completely different direction. If she does, he swore, I'll kill her with my bare hands.

"How badly can you hurt Bran? He'd probably treat it as a valuable experience for his acting career. But no, I don't think she's going to stay with him. And chances are she'll be the one who says goodbye." She snorted. "Debbie's *always* the one to say goodbye."

Keith looked hard at Bran, so carefree and happy. I don't want you to get hurt, Bran.

"Come on," Keith said, offering Laura his hand. "Can I offer you a coke and some of those meatballs?"

"Sounds good,' Laura said, standing up and smoothing out her skirt. "Lead on."

CHAPTER TEN

Later in the evening, Keith decided that he had to get some air. The party had broken up into couples and small groups; he didn't want to face Laura again for a while, and he certainly wasn't going to sit with Bran and Debbie, not when the two of them were acting like they were pairing off to board Noah's Ark. So he calmly let himself out the back door and stood in the yard, looking up at the sky.

It wasn't a very friendly sky—low clouds blotted out all the light of stars and moon, and the trees rustled ominously. Keith pulled his knit cap further down over his ears. It was getting colder. Maybe there would even be a storm before the night was out.

"What are you doing out here?" Bran said, hopping out of the back door. He was alone; Keith was glad, because he didn't think he could deal with Debbie right now.

"Just getting a breath of fresh air."

"Sounds good to me." Bran showed the effects of all the beer he'd drunk…he was unsteady on his feet and there was a curious thickness in his voice. "Do you want to go for a walk in the woods?"

"It's pretty cold out here," Keith said dubiously.

"Come on." Bran tugged at his arm, pulling him toward the woods. Keith shrugged and went along.

"How far back do these woods go?" Keith asked as they started into the trees.

Bran shrugged. "I don't know. Good mile or so, I guess. There are paths." He kicked at some loose dirt. "Used to play back here all the time when I was a little kid."

"You've known Debbie that long?"

"Oh, yeah." Bran led the way to a tiny clearing, where he leaned against a wide oak tree. Floodlights from Debbie's house made strange patterns of light and shadow across his face and jacket. "My parents were friends with the Vovcenkos before I even came along. Used to have some really great times with Debbie and her sister." He frowned, looked back toward the house. "That was before Debbie started acting so weird."

"Hey, look," Keith said, "I don't want to pry into your—"

"That's how everybody feels. Let me tell you something, Keith my boy." Bran waved a finger in Keith's direction. "Sometimes things ain't what they seem. Everybody has this idea that Debbie and I are going together—even Debbie thinks so now. And it just isn't so."

"Okay," Keith said, trying to sound nonchalant.

"Oh, hell." Bran shook his head. "If I wasn't so drunk, I wouldn't be saying any of this."

"It's okay. I won't tell."

Bran reached for Keith, rubbed his shoulder affectionately. "I know you won't. You're probably the only one I can count on. And you know why?"

"Why"

"Because you're a good friend, that's why."

Keith forced a laugh. "I try hard." He wasn't at all comfortable with Bran in this condition. Suppose something bad happened—Bran could fall and break a leg, or cut himself, and Keith would have to run back to the house for help. "Hey, don't you think we should go back now?"

"Not yet. I don't want to have to play up to Debbie, not now. I've been doing it all night." Bran cocked his head at Keith. "Poor Keith, sober with all these drunks around, and now you're thinking that you wish I would shut up and let you go get warm."

"No," Keith said automatically.

Bran was suddenly serious, as he leaned close to Keith. The smell of beer on Bran's breath was almost overpowering.

"I brought you back here because this is where we always used to tell secrets, when we were kids. I've got to talk to somebody, Keith, and like I say, you're the only one I can trust."

"What?"

"Look, it's about Debbie. I guess you think we're a couple too, just like everybody else?"

"I *did*. But you just said you weren't. So why do you—?"

"Keep hanging around her? Like I said, Debbie and I are friends from way back. If she wants everybody else to think that she's my girl, well, I guess I can help her out." Bran lowered his eyes. "Besides, that way nobody wonders about me."

"What are you trying to tell me?"

"Nobody wonders about Bran. Bran's with Debbie, nobody thinks that Bran might be wishing he was with somebody else."

Keith's heart stopped. With an effort of will, he forced himself to take a breath, then another. "Who?"

"Warren."

Keith looked away. He didn't trust himself; his emotions were written all over his face. "W-What's wrong with that?" Inside, he thought: So Debbie was right. It wasn't just malicious gossip.

"You don't understand. Warren isn't...well, let's just say that he isn't one of the most understanding people in the world. If he knew how I feel, he'd treat it as a personal attack. Things could get pretty ugly."

"What, you think he'd hit you or something?"

"Worse. It could break up the group. Warren wouldn't want anything to do with me. I'm not sure what Jane and Rick would do, but I think they'd go with Warren. Laura and Bert would stick with me, no matter what they thought. Debbie...I don't know. I don't like to think about it."

"Bran, it's none of their business if you like boys. Jeez, who do they think they are?"

"It's not liking boys that's the problem. It's liking Warren."
Bran sighed. "This is hard to explain, you haven't been around
so you don't know what's been happening. It's like this—
beginning of last year, Dale Sullivan made a pass at Warren.
This was before Dale and Mark Greenberg started hanging
around together."

"So what happened?"

"You don't see Dale and Mark spending much time with
us, do you?"

"They were at the football game the other day."

"Everybody was at the football game. But Dale and Mark,
they're just not part of the group any more. They used to be.
Now every time they come up in conversation, Warren goes
out of his way to tell us all how much he hates Dale."

Light dawned, and Keith felt a sudden surge of sympathy
for Bran. "And you don't want Warren to hate *you*."

"Exactly."

"So what are you going to do?"

"Keep going on the way I have been. Soon enough we're
going to graduate, and then we'll be going our separate ways
to college. Then it won't matter. I just want the group to stay
together as long as it can, that's all."

Keith frowned. "Well that's no fun. Meanwhile, you're
going through hell. I don't think that's right."

"Let me show you something." Bran dug into his pocket,
pulled out his keys. "Can you see the keychain?"

On the end of the chain was a small round piece of metal.
Keith held it into a patch of light, saw the familiar design of
comedy and tragedy masks. "Yeah."

"That's the symbol of the Thespian Society," Bran said.
"Can you read the motto?"

The light was poor. "No."

Bran straightened up. "'Act well your part, there all the
honor lies,'" he quoted. "It means that you have to take all the
parts that are given to you, and play them to the best of your
ability. This is a part I have to play."

Keith handed the keychain back. "Well I'm sorry, I think that your happiness is more important than some dumb motto. You should at least tell him how you feel."

Bran sighed. "You've never been in the situation, or you'd know what I'm saying. It's just not worth it, Keith." He squeezed Keith's shoulder again. "Anyway, it's good to have somebody to talk to. Do you mind if I come to you sometimes, just to talk?"

"Of course not."

"Good." Bran shivered. "Hey, let's get back. I have to take a piss something wicked."

Once they were back at the house, Keith sat on the basement stairs and watched Bran. What a bizarre situation, he thought. I'm in love with Bran, and he's in love with Warren. And Debbie, nobody knows what Debbie really wants.

I just don't want him to get hurt.

And...I'm afraid he's going to.

*

Keith's mind was in turmoil when he arrived home that night. Sitting up in bed, with his blanket pulled around him and a fierce storm brewing outside his window, he let his thoughts race past without attempting to tie them down.

Bran is in love with Warren. He likes boys! So I have a chance.

Keith shook his head. Don't be silly, he told himself. He loves Warren, not you. You're his friend...a friend that he trusts with something he hasn't told anybody else...but still just a friend. Outside, the wind roared and a patter of heavy raindrops began on the roof. Keith shivered. He loves somebody else.

Stop it, he chided himself. Think of how poor Bran feels. You think *you're* miserable, imagine Bran: for him it's been going on...how long? Years? And he's had to face more agony than you ever have. How terrible it must be, to know that you could never tell the person you loved how you felt. At least I *could* tell Bran, Keith thought, and he wouldn't hate me for it.

He hugged his pillow and felt warm tears fill his eyes, overflow down his cheeks. After a few minutes, Keith curled up into a ball and sobbed to himself.

Outside, the storm wailed.

*

After Saturday's performance, the cast members all went to dinner at the local McDonald's. Everyone still had traces of makeup on, Jane and Debbie had their hair sprayed grey, and there was a constant interchange of lines from the play to disturb the quiet of the night. Keith felt a little sorry for the people who worked at McDonald's—but he was also caught up in the exhilaration, and he didn't waste too much sympathy on them.

Mostly, he watched Bran. The older boy did his usual sitting with Debbie, casually draping his arm around her, and a little bit of harmless kissing. But now that Keith knew what to look for, he saw how Bran's clear brown eyes always strayed in Warren's direction, how Bran absent-mindedly paid attention to Debbie while his real concern was with Warren.

And Warren, of course, ignored Bran most of the night.

Bran drove several kids home, arranging the drop-offs so that he and Keith were alone in the car at the end. Bran didn't say anything as he pulled the car up to Keith's house and killed the motor; he just raised an eyebrow. Keith sat back in his seat and sighed heavily.

"How can he behave like that to you?" Keith asked suddenly. "If he paid any attention at all he'd know what was going on, and you'd think he'd have the decency to—"

"Hey, don't get worked up, kid. I'm used to it. I think I do a pretty good job of hiding my feelings when Warren's around." He flashed an apologetic grin. "I think I'm that much of an actor."

"Oh, you're great. But I know what to look for, and I see everything now. God, Bran, how long can you go on hurting like that?"

"I'm not hurting all that much. At least I know there's never going to be any chance of anything happening between us."

"Don't you…dream about it?"

Bran looked away. "Constantly. I've got a pretty active imagination."

A sudden rush of emotions swept over Keith—anger, pain, love, desire—and he reached out to Bran laid his hand on the other boy's shoulder. "I'm sorry."

"Sorry? It's not your fault."

Keith thought he should move his hand, should take it back lest Bran feel the tightly-controlled tension, the awful passion smoldering below the surface of his skin. But he was frozen like a little kid who just knocked over a lamp…even if he willed his hand to move he didn't think his muscles would obey him.

Bran's trying to pretend that he's not bothered. That he's just acting a part. But I know better. I can sense what he's feeling underneath that shell.

"I'm sorry," Keith said, "that I can't be Warren." *Thank you, Frank,* he thought, *for giving me just the right thing to say.*

Bran patted Keith's hand. "Thanks. You don't have to be Warren. Just be yourself. That's all I want you to be."

After that, Bran didn't mention their conversation in the woods, and Keith was a little shy about bringing up the point. But during the next week there were several times, at lunch or during before-school study sessions, when Keith caught Bran looking at Warren with hunger in his eyes, and Keith felt for him.

Keith himself didn't know what to think or do. In seventh grade he had seen a movie about the survivors of the Hiroshima atomic bombing—for the rest of his life he would remember the empty eyes of those haunted souls, the expressions of people whose world had been completely destroyed in one instant of sun-bright fire. He felt a little bit like one of those people, now: Bran's confession had left him shell-shocked and he needed time to recover.

He thought that his mother knew something had happened, but kept herself from asking out of respect for his privacy. Once or twice he started downstairs to tell her, then turned around and sat back down at his desk to stare out the window. He knew what she would say: that he ought to go after what would make him happy. And he couldn't. Not when Bran was hurting, not when it would seem like trying to take unfair advantage of the other boy.

No, Keith thought—I won't tell him how I feel. He needs a friend now, one who isn't going to be threatening, one who will listen and give sympathy. I don't know how he's managed to go all this time without anybody to talk to. It must have been awful.

I can't *be* Warren for him, and I certainly can't make Warren love him. But I can be the best friend possible, can listen to him and give him whatever positive response there is to offer. That won't help. It won't ease his pain at all. But it's the only thing I can do.

Monday and Tuesday after school the cast was busy dismantling the set and storing away all the costumes. The play was a wild success; it had earned well over two thousand dollars for the Drama Club, and Mr. Hening was talking about a picnic later in the month. Keith enjoyed taking the set apart, but he felt a little sad...now that the play was over, and there wouldn't be another one until spring, he wouldn't see Bran as often.

Sure enough, on Wednesday Keith rode the bus home, just like the old days, and let himself into the empty house after a cold walk from the bus stop. He did his homework quickly, then tried watching television—but none of the programs caught his attention. He knew what was wrong: he was telling himself that he ought to be at play practice, and he felt guilty because he wasn't.

Finally, bored, he picked up the phone and carefully dialed Frank's number. Frank answered, and sounded astonished to hear Keith's voice. "So, why this surprise?" Frank asked.

"I'm bored," Keith said. "We've finished rehearsal and I'm home early. I thought I'd call and see how you were."

"Doing fine." He could see Frank's nod. "How about you? Hanging in there?"

"Uh-huh."

"What about Bran? Any news on that front?"

"Yeah." Keith told Frank about Bran's confession. "He told me not to tell anybody, but he means anybody around here. I guess you're safe to tell. And I wanted your opinion."

"Hey, it sounds good to me. This is what you were wondering, right? Does he like boys, or doesn't he? Well, now you know. Go for it, Keith. Tell him that you're in love with him and see what happens from there."

"I can't. It would be like…betraying a trust." Keith thought back to the sensitivity game of person-in-the-middle. Blind-folded, Bran was falling back toward him—it was Keith's duty not to step aside, not to give the other boy any surprises.

"If he had any taste at all, Keith, he'd be going after you instead of Warren anyhow."

"Thanks. That's very flattering. But it doesn't get me anywhere."

"Well, what *have* you told Bran?"

Keith lowered his head. "I told him that he should tell Warren how he feels, because he can't keep going on the way he is."

"Isn't that just what *you're* doing, though? Why don't you take your own advice, fella?"

"I can't."

There was silence for a few long seconds, then Frank sighed. "You know what I think, Keith?"

"What?"

"I think you're just afraid."

"Of what?"

"Of having him reject you. It's not a nice thing, to open yourself up to someone and be vulnerable, if they might say 'no' and leave you hurting."

Keith thought about it.

"Keith? You there?"

"I'm here. I think you may be right—partly. But suppose I say the hell with rejection, and I go ahead and tell him I love him. And then he decides that he doesn't want to be close to me anymore? I…I don't want to lose him, Frank."

"Worry about losing him when you've *got* him. Don't panic about it now when you hardly have anything to lose." Frank laughed. "Remember what Coach Russell told us in gym class? 'No pain, no gain.' Remember how many times we tried out before he got parts in plays? You have to be a little vulnerable, sometimes, and risk losing things."

"You sound like Mom."

"You're mom's a smart woman, Keith. You should listen to her. Listen to me."

"I don't know."

"Think about it. Hey, your mom isn't going to be too happy with you running up her phone bill."

"You're right. Thanks, Frank. I'll think about what you said. Really I will."

"Good. Love you."

"Love you too. Bye."

Keith hung up the phone, then sat for fifteen minutes staring at it.

Something…something had to happen soon.

CHAPTER ELEVEN

"The one I'm worried about is Debbie," Keith said, dipping a cookie in his milk and taking a large bite.

Keith and Bran were sitting in Keith's kitchen after school on Thursday. Bran had taken Keith home, and stopped in for a snack; in the course of demolishing half a jar of chocolate chip cookies and two pints of milk, they started discussing their friends. One thing led to another, and soon the whole issue of Bran and Warren and Debbie came up.

"What makes you say that?" Bran asked.

"Don't take this wrong. But you're not treating her right. She thinks you're her boyfriend."

Bran frowned. "I beg to differ, my good man. Debbie knows what's going on. She figured it out a while ago. Surely you're heard her talking about it."

"Well...as a matter of fact, she did say that you had the hots for Warren. But I think she was kidding."

"She's said it often enough."

"Have you talked to her about it?"

"No. It's gotten back to me what she's been saying. If she has me figured out, then she ought to know I'm not her boyfriend." Bran sighed. "In a way, we're both using one another. I'm using Debbie to keep people from wondering about me, and Debbie's using me to make other guys notice her. I guess she thinks people are jealous of me."

"I still don't know," Keith said. "It seems to me that you're not really playing fair with her."

"And she's not playing fair with me. We'll get by, kid. Debbie can take care of herself."

"If you say so."

"Hey," Bran said, looking at the kitchen clock, "I'd love to stay and chat, but I have to get home and start something for dinner."

"Your Dad doesn't cook?" Keith asked, helping Bran into his jacket.

"Dad's idea of a gourmet meal is putting frozen dinners in the oven and eating in front of the TV. I can't cook real well, but I can read recipes and Mother had a lot of cookbooks. I usually cook a meal two or three times a week."

"No wonder you like Mom's cookies so much. We'll have to invite you over to dinner again."

"Sounds good to me." At the door, Bran stopped. "Did Bob tell your class about the picnic?"

"Yes." The Drama Club was having a picnic at the State Park on Saturday, to be paid for with profits from the play.

"You gonna be there?"

"Of course. You?"

"Wouldn't miss it." Bran saluted. "Take care, kid. See you in school tomorrow."

"Bye."

*

Friday night the gang went to the movies. Due to some obscure rotation schedule that Keith didn't understand, it was Jane's turn to pick the movie—so they wound up at a slasher film complete with a mumbling maniac killer and pretty, innocent victims. Keith sat between Bran and Laura, and he squeezed Laura's hand as often as she squeezed his. Bran seemed quite unaffected by the violence and blood, going so far as to cheer the killer in one particularly gruesome scene.

Afterward they stopped at McDonald's for food, and it was the same story as usual: Bran mooned over Warren, with no one but Keith aware of what he was doing. Keith paid particular attention to Debbie, trying to decide once and for all if she really know what she had gotten herself into.

He came away unsure.

When he came home, Keith found a letter waiting for him, addressed in Frank's scrawling handwriting. He tore it open and found a greeting card with a picture of a bizarre monkey hanging by one hand from a tree branch while he reached for a banana with the other. Inside the card said, "Go for it!" Beneath the message Frank had scribbled, "Good luck with Bran."

Keith smiled, then shook his head.

"Something wrong?" Mom asked, looking up from her book.

"Just Frank and his sense of humor." Keith sighed. "Have to be up early for the picnic tomorrow. I'm going to bed."

"Oh. Goodnight, then."

"Goodnight." Keith looked again at the card. That Frank!

*

Although it was the third week in November, the weather was remarkably good; the air was crisp but the sun was shining brightly, and when Keith rolled out of bed at eight o'clock he quickly pulled the curtains closed.

By nine-thirty Bran showed up, car already full. Keith took his place in the back seat, with Laura half on his lap, and they roared off toward the State Park.

Luckily, it wasn't a long trip—they arrived within half an hour. It took only a few minutes to find the picnic spot that the Drama Club had rented. When they located it, Laura squealed in joy. There were some picnic tables, and a large stone barbecue in which some of the seniors were already building a fire; beyond the tables the land dropped toward the river, and the view was spectacular.

"When do we eat?" Bert asked after saying hello to the other drama people.

Bob Hening playfully batted Bert on the head with a bag of hamburger rolls. "Not for a few hours yet, Stage Manager. Don't you think everybody should work up an appetite now?"

Bran ran to the edge, where a steep incline descended into trees and huge rocks. "I know what *I'm* going to do," he shouted. "I'm going to climb down to the river. Anybody who wants can follow me."

Laura chased after him, Warren followed, and Debbie gave a sigh. "I'm glad I wore an old pair of pants, I'm going to get filthy. Coming, Bert?" She started down the incline.

Bert shrugged. "Food later, I guess. Come on, Keith, let's see if we can keep them from breaking their fool necks."

"I think it's kind of neat," Keith said, starting carefully down the slope. He had to proceed slowly, gripping tree branches and digging his fingers into cracks in the rocks. By the time he reached the bottom, a climb of about fifteen minutes, he was glad to stop and rest. The others were all sitting down, panting, when he arrived; Bran looked up.

"Where's Bert?"

"He's on his way. Whew, that was some climb."

Bran gave a fiendish grin. "Wait until we go back," he said wickedly.

Debbie groaned.

They played around the river for a good hour and a half. Warren discovered a snake, and Laura stood barefoot in the frigid water just to prove that she could do it, but otherwise their time was filled with exploring, skipping stones across the river, and trying to find an easier way up the hill.

Eventually Keith shrugged his shoulders and started up the slope the way they'd come. "I'm getting hungry," he said. "Somebody has to start back, it might as well be me."

It took longer to go up than it had to come down, but eventually they were all back at the picnic tables. Jane had her guitar and a crowd of admirers, so Keith settled down with Laura and Bert to listen. Bran went off with Debbie and Warren to toss horseshoes.

Lunch was informal, roughly organized by Jerry Todd and his friends; Keith went back to the barbecue twice before his stomach felt full. Then he sat in the sun and watched some of the girls throw bread at birds.

Bran, meanwhile, settled down at a picnic table with Debbie and Warren. From where he sat Keith couldn't hear what they were saying, but he saw the direction of everyone's eyes. Always the same thing. Bran sneaking sidelong glances at Warren. Debbie looking toward Bran. Warren gazing off into the distance. Laura, wherever she was, wishing she could be with Bran. And Keith himself: watching Bran. As usual.

Keith sighed, picked himself up, and headed into the trees. He didn't know where he was going, he just wanted to get away from the gang for a while. He walked aimlessly, pausing now and again to scrape his feet in the layer of dead leaves that covered the ground. His mind raced, but not with any coherent thoughts. He wasn't thinking, just letting his mind run in whatever courses it wished.

He found a fallen log and sat down on it. The sun was getting lower in the sky, but its light still streamed brightly through bare branches. A flock of birds flew by overhead, and once Keith glimpsed a squirrel dashing up a tree.

When he was almost ready to go back and join the others, he heard someone walking toward him.

Bran.

"Hi," Bran said. "What'cha doing?"

"Just sitting."

Bran sat next to him and looked into Keith's eyes. For a moment Keith was reminded of the day on the lighting deck, when they'd played the game of staring at one another. I wondered then if you could read my thoughts, Bran. Can you?

"You don't seem happy," Bran said.

Keith raised an eyebrow. And should I tell you what's bothering me?

Mom thinks I should. Frank thinks I should. And I've been telling you that you should tell Warren how you feel—isn't it the same thing?

"Oh, I don't know," Keith said. "Not unhappy…just, well, a little bothered."

"Poor Keith. Everybody comes to you with their problems, but we never ask if we can help you. What's bothering you, kid?"

"You and Warren. And Debbie. I just…just couldn't sit around any more and watch you hurting. So I decided to take a walk."

"You're too good to me, kid. Everybody hurts. You care. Why?"

"I'm your friend."

"Well, hey, I really appreciate it. But you've got to stop letting this get you down. It's my problem. Don't be so sympathetic."

Keith took a deep breath. All right, Frank. Trembling, he said, "Bran…I care so much because I know just how you feel. I feel the same way."

Concern crossed Bran's face, and he put a comforting hand on Keith's shoulder. Keith flinched.

"Who is it?" Bran asked.

Keith swallowed, looked away. "You."

Bran froze, pulled back a trifle. "Oh, God," he said softly. "And you've sat there and let me babble about Warren." Bran deliberately put both arms around Keith, pulled him close. "You poor boy. Poor, faithful friend. I'm so sorry."

"Don't be. I…I just hope that this doesn't cause trouble."

"How could it cause trouble?" Bran held Keith at arm's length, looked into his eyes. "I love you, kid."

"Warren —" Keith whispered.

"Warren I can never have. But if you…."

Keith turned his head away. "Don't."

"Look at me."

Keith turned back, met Bran's gaze. Then, holding him securely, Bran bent his head nearer and their lips met.

Keith almost couldn't believe what was happening. For an instant he thought it was a dream, or a cruel trick, but then he hugged Bran tight and Bran hugged him back, and he knew it was real.

Bran kissed him again, this time harder, more demanding. Bran put one hand behind Keith's head, and stroked his hair as he pressed his lips to Keith's.

As one, the boys opened their lips, and Keith felt the exciting touch of Bran's tongue on his lips, exploring the inside of his mouth—and then Bran forcefully pulled Keith's tongue into his own mouth, engulfing Keith in warm, passionate wetness.

The kiss went on for eternity, became something tender and playful. In a few minutes Keith found himself half-laying on the log, with his head against Bran's chest and the older boy's arms around him. Bran sighed.

"How long have you been in love with me, you little brat?"

"S-since I first met you, outside the auditorium."

"And you haven't told me?"

"I didn't know how you'd react."

Bran kissed him again, turned Keith's head and gently nibbled at the place where his chin met his earlobe. At the same time, Bran rubbed his hands up and down Keith's back forcefully, stroking and embracing at the same time. Keith made a sound that was halfway between a sigh and a moan.

Bran grinned. "Does that let you know how I react?"

"I...guess so."

Bran hugged Keith again, then stood up. "Much more of this, kid, and I'm going to wind up raping you in the woods. Let's go back and join the others."

Part of Keith wanted to stay, to keep doing what he was doing with Bran and see where it would take them. But the more sensible part of him took command and made him stand up and brush his hair back into place.

After a few minutes walking, Keith stopped. Bran gave him a quizzical look. "What?"

"Are we going to tell the others?"

Bran shrugged. "Why bother? They'll figure it out soon enough. They might as well have the chance to gossip about us."

Keith smiled and held out his hand. Bran took it, and hand in hand they strolled back to the picnic tables and the rest of the gang.

*

"Let's see," Laura said, ticking off on her fingers. "Jane thinks you're cute, Bert doesn't care, Warren grunts a lot, and Debbie thinks it's disgusting." She moved up in line with her tray, and Keith followed. It was lunchtime, Monday, and Keith had dragged Laura into the lunch line so he could talk with her.

"Debbie said that?"

Laura nodded. "Well *I* think it's dis*gust*ing," she said, in perfect imitation of Debbie's tone. "I mean, can't they have the decency to do that sort of thing in private? Do they *have* to come strolling out of the woods holding hands?" Laura wagged a finger, still doing Debbie. "Mark my words, no good is going to come of this. Bad enough that Bran should suddenly decide he likes boys, but he has to choose *Keith*, of all people."

"Did she say what was wrong with me?"

Laura shrugged. "You're only a junior. And you're new… lower than low, according to Debbie. Without us, you wouldn't be anything." She held up her hands as if to ward off a blow. "I'm just telling you what she said."

"What do *you* think, Laura?"

Laura tossed her head. "Me? I think it's wonderful." She sighed. "Oh, I'd rather that Bran decided to go with me— but I can take it if he's not interested. I guess I'm a little jealous of you. A tiny bit. But the two of you look happy, and that's the important thing, isn't it?"

Keith nodded.

"You are happy, aren't you?"

"Me? Yes. Bran...I don't know." I wonder, Keith thought, if he is just doing this to make me happy. If he's wishing all the time that I was Warren.

The line moved forward, they got lunch, and went to sit down at the table. Keith sat next to Bran, in the position that used to be Debbie's; Debbie was on the other side of the table, talking to Jane, and she made quite a show of ignoring Keith and Bran.

After lunch, Bran walked with Keith as far as his next class.

"Do you think Debbie's going to be okay?" Keith asked.

"Sure," Bran answered with a smile. "She just needs a little bit of time to get things sorted out in her head."

"I hope you're right."

"Here's my class." Bran leaned over, kissed Keith lightly on the cheek, then said, "See you after school. Have a good afternoon."

"Bye," Keith answered automatically. Then, distracted, he wandered to his history class and lost himself in a discussion about President Jefferson.

CHAPTER TWELVE

Monday night after dinner, Keith was just reaching to pick up the phone when it rang, making him jump.

"Hello?"

"Keith, buddy."

"Bran. I was just going to call you. What's up?"

"Want to go to a movie Friday?" Thursday was Thanksgiving; school was closed Thursday and Friday.

"I just finished talking to Mom about Thanksgiving. What are you doing on Thursday?"

Bran sighed. "Dad and I have been invited to the Vovcenkos for dinner, so I guess I'm going there. I can't say I'm too happy with the idea. I can't see Debbie and me sitting around watching the football games arm-in-arm the way we did last year."

"Mom and I are cooking turkey and all the trimmings... she wants to know if you're free to come over here. It'll be just the three of us."

Bran was silent for a minute. "I don't know. I'll have to talk to Dad about it."

"Well, if you don't want to..." Keith started, trying to keep from sounding hurt. "I know it's awfully short notice."

"No, it's not that. I just have to check with Dad, that's all."

"Okay. You can call me back when you find out. Now what's this about a movie Friday?"

"Well, I thought you might want to do something when we're off. Like a date, I guess. A movie seemed the proper thing to suggest."

Keith chuckled. "Yes, do let's be proper. Sure. I picked the film last time, why don't you decide this time?"

Keith heard newspaper rustling in the background, and Bran murmured "whoops" once. "Hold on," he said.

After a few seconds Bran came back. "Sorry about that. I had to get the movie section. It looks like a choice between sorority girls, divorce, or that new spy film. I vote for spies."

Keith shrugged. "I don't have any interest in sorority girls, and divorce sounds depressing. Spies it is, then."

"Good, we'll plan on that, and I'll get back to you on Thursday as soon as Dad comes home."

"Sounds good. Bye, Bran."

"Bye, kid."

*

Keith tried not to be anxious, but all evening he kept looking toward the phone as if he could make it ring by willing it. The phone, of course, didn't cooperate.

It wasn't until nine o'clock, when Keith and his mother were settling down with a bowl of fresh popcorn to watch television, that Bran called back.

"Hiya, kid. Sorry to keep you waiting. Dad just came in half an hour ago, and I broached the subject of Thanksgiving."

"And?"

Bran lowered his voice. "Can't say that he's too happy with the idea of me not going to Debbie's. Personally, though, I don't care what he thinks. So if the offer is still open, I'd love to come over for dinner. Can I get there early and help you guys fix it?"

"Sure the offer's open. Hold on, I'll ask." Keith covered the mouthpiece, leaned his head into the living room. "It's Bran, about Thursday. He wants to know if he can come over early and help us fix dinner."

Mom laughed. "I can't promise him that basting a turkey and making sauerkraut will be all that exciting, but it that's what he wants to do, then of course."

"Thanks." Back to Bran, Keith said, "Mom says that's fine." He took a breath, his hands suddenly shaking. "And Bran...Mom said it would be okay if...if you wanted to spend the night."

"Oh."

"Don't feel pressured."

"I guess I *could* do that, couldn't I?"

"Well, don't feel like you have to, I just thought...."

"Kid, you have the strangest way of making a proposition. If that's what you're doing. My good man, I will be delighted to spend the night Thursday. Maybe we can sleep in and go to our movie right from your house, then."

"Fine."

"Good, then. See you in school."

"See you. Bye."

Keith hung up the phone, then leaned against the wall in relief. He didn't know what he was getting himself into, didn't know what would come of this—but the first hurdle was passed.

Only now, he thought, how will I last until Thursday?

*

When Keith arrived home from school on Tuesday, he immediately went to the basement and started unpacking, one by one, the boxes that were still piled up from the move. They contained a vast assortment of things: spare curtains, summer clothes, old toys, books...all things that he and his mother had not managed to unpack yet.

By the time Mom came home he had reduced the pile by almost one-third. She stood with her hands on her hips and whistled. "Great job, son. Where did you get the energy for all this?"

Keith grinned wryly. "I have to have some project to keep me busy between now and Thursday. Might as well be useful."

Mom sat down on the steps, cocked her head. "I hope you're not going to get too serious about Bran."

"What do you mean? A week ago you were telling me that I should...get involved with him." Keith busied himself with another box, hoping he wouldn't have to look his mother in the eyes. He wasn't ashamed, it was just...embarrassing.

"I want you to be happy. But I also don't want you to get so serious that you let yourself in for being hurt too much. You have to have a sense of proportion. It's only been three days...."

Keith took out extra plates and transferred them to the box he had set aside to go to the kitchen. "How do you know if you're getting too serious?"

"There's no easy way." She sighed. "Maybe I don't know what I'm talking about. I want to see you happy, Keith, and I guess I'm just a little nervous. I've never been in this situation before."

"W-would you rather Bran didn't come over Thursday?"

"Of course not."

"Would you rather...he didn't stay overnight?"

Mom sighed deeply. "Now you're striking below the belt. I don't know how to answer that question. I'd rather my little boy wasn't growing up so fast. But I know what young men are like, and I know that sooner or later you two will...."

"Uh-huh," Keith said, keeping his eyes averted.

"And I guess I'd rather that you knew there was some place where you could feel safe and comfortable."

"Mom," Keith said, turning to face her. "I...thank you." He hugged her, then picked up the kitchen box. "I've got to get this stuff put away."

"Right." She wiped her eyes, then clapped him on the shoulder. "And I've got to get something started for dinner. Let's go."

*

Wednesday night the weather turned cold. When Keith awoke in the middle of the night, frost had painted lacy designs on his window and he heard the heat pipes groaning to themselves. In the morning it was windy and deliciously cold; Keith ran out to get the paper and was happy to get back into the warm house.

The turkey went in early, and then Keith turned on the TV and he and his mother settled down to watch parades. It was about ten o'clock when Bran pulled up and dashed from his car to the door; Keith helped him in and took his jacket.

"What should I do with my stuff?" Bran asked, holding up a small overnight bag.

"What's in there?"

"Toothbrush, a new shirt, underwear, all that kind of stuff."

"Oh. Just put it on the steps, we can take it upstairs to my room later." He called to his mother: "Bran's here!"

"Good," she said, rubbing her hands together. "Now we can start getting the work done. Bran, do you peel potatoes?"

"Just lead me to 'em."

"Good. By the time you have the potatoes peeled, I should have the sauerkraut on and be ready to start cooking them. Bran, I hope you like pineapple upside-down cake, because that's what we're having for dessert."

"I love it, Mrs. Graff. What, no pumpkin pie or mince-meat?"

Mom shook her head. "Too traditional. Besides, when Keith was little he wouldn't eat pumpkin pie, and he picked mincemeat to pieces before he'd touch it. In the interests of sanity, his father and I turned to pineapple upside-down cake. It seemed like a good compromise."

"You don't like pumpkin pie?" Bran said to Keith in disbelief.

Keith spread his hands. "So sue me." He handed Bran the potato peeler, took a paring knife from the utility drawer. "Let's get started on those potatoes."

There was enough work to keep everyone busy, and when dinner was finally ready Keith was more than ready to eat.

Conversation was light—Mom talked about the play and encouraged Bran to relate stories about rehearsals; Bran in turn asked Keith and his mother about Kinwood and they fell into discussion of the differences between there and Oak Grove. Soon enough, without Keith even noticing that time had passed, dessert was on the table and he was showing Bran how to make whipped cream with the electric mixer.

It took another hour or so until the dishes were cleared away and carefully stacked in the dishwasher. When Keith finally took out the garbage, the sky was streaked with the last rosy light of day, and a few brave stars already poked their heads out from behind clouds. He stopped and looked at one of them, whispered a childhood rhyme.

"Star light, star bright, first star I see tonight...."

I want him to love me, he thought. That's my wish. So far, he's doing this because I love him, and he's being nice to me. I want him to love me for myself, not because he feels sorry for me. I want him to fall in love with me the way I have with him.

Is that too much to ask?

The stars brightened and Keith, shivering, went inside.

Later that night, when Mrs. Graff was settled in her room on the phone with her mother, and the last of the Thanksgiving specials on TV was over, Bran stretched and yawned. "I think it's getting to be that time, Kid," he said with a smile.

"Yeah," Keith replied through a throat that had suddenly become very dry. Maybe, he thought, we can just go to sleep. Maybe I'm wrong about this whole thing. Maybe....

Bran leaned over and kissed him briefly on the lips. "You look about as nervous as I was the first time I went on stage. Don't worry. This isn't a performance."

Keith swallowed. "Okay." He turned off the TV and started up the stairs. Bran picked up his overnight bag and followed. "This is my room," Keith said, "And that's the bathroom. This room is going to be Mom's office if we can ever get enough time to get it set up."

Bran entered Keith's room and looked around approvingly. "I like it. It's bigger than my room." He put his bag down on the desk, sat down on the bed and took off his shoes. "This is a cozy room, Keith. I like the color." The walls were a pastel red, nearly orange.

"Thanks. Mom gave me a choice of four; this was the one I liked best."

"Relax." Bran patted the mattress next to him. "Here, sit down."

Keith sat, and Bran slipped an arm around him. "Hey," Bran said, "You're shaking. Are you scared?"

"I'm ch-chilly."

"Poor kid. Here, let me warm you up." Bran rubbed his arms, hugged him tighter. Keith held on to Bran, then buried his face in the older boy's shoulder.

Bran rubbed his own cheek against Keith's, a firm, slightly rough pressure that stirred warmth in Keith and made him draw his breath sharply. Then Bran continued the movement of his face, kissed Keith's neck and dug his chin into the hollow where the younger boy's shoulders me his neck.

Bran's mouth was warm, wet, and demanding; Keith felt himself settle back against the bed until he lay full length, Bran's body pressed against his, half on top of him. Bran continued to kiss him, now nibbling gently, now nuzzling Keith with feather-gentle touches of his lips on tight, excited skin.

"Warmer?" Bran said, looking into Keith's eyes.

"Uh-hmm." Keith reached up to touch Bran's face. I can't believe he's actually here, he thought, as he ran his fingertips gently over Bran's forehead, eyebrows, and lips. He stroked

Bran's hair, and Bran slowly lowered his face until his lips touched Keith's.

Now they kissed, and Keith was no longer afraid. He parted his lips, ran his tongue over Bran's teeth, let the older boy enter his mouth. Then, hugging Bran as tight as we could, running his hands over Bran's back, Keith turned his attention to his friend's neck, and kissed Bran as Bran had kissed him. Bran stiffened, gasped, and smiled.

Keith grinned and attacked Bran's ear. Careful with his teeth, he licked Bran's earlobe, massaging it with his lips. Bran moaned with pleasure.

"Where did you learn that?" Bran said, sounding surprised.

"My friend Frank," Keith said. "Does it bother you?"

"Bother me? God, no. You're hot, kid. Damn hot."

"I try hard."

Keith continued his attention to Bran's ears, alternating back and forth with slow, sensual kisses. After a bit of this, Bran grabbed Keith and pinned him down on the bed, started nibbling at his neck.

Rather than the pain he expected, Keith felt an almost unbearable pleasure—pleasure that electrified his whole body, made all his muscles tighten. He hugged Bran and grunted.

Bran, making a noise halfway between a laugh and a growl, ran his hands over Keith's chest as he kissed him. Then, without warning, he started unfastening the buttons of Keith's shirt. In a few seconds, Keith's chest was bare.

The touch of Bran's hands on his skin was both delight and torment. Keith wriggled helplessly, knotting his fingers in Bran's hair. Bran kissed his neck, then moved down and bestowed a fiery kiss on Keith's right nipple. Keith arched his back and groaned. "Oh my God."

Bran looked up and grinned a self-satisfied grin. "You like that, eh?"

"I..." Keith couldn't speak as Bran returned to the business at hand. Finally, when he couldn't take any more,

Keith wrestled Bran to the mattress and pulled the older boy's shirt over his head, throwing it to the floor.

"Let's see how you like it." Keith bowed his head and ran his tongue along the firm, slightly downy surface of Bran's chest, until he reached one of the boy's nipples. He kissed the tiny mound, and was rewarded with a spasm of pleasure from Bran. He continued while Bran stroked his head and his back.

For the moment exhausted, the two boys lay peacefully next to one another, legs entwined and chests pressed firmly together. Bran lightly stroked Keith's hair, and Keith kissed Bran on the cheek.

"Are you happy?" Bran asked.

"Ecstatic. How about you."

"I never dreamed." Bran sighed. "I was a fool, kid. All this time, this is what I wanted with Warren, what I could never have…and it never dawned on me that there might be someone else who could give me this kind of love."

"I'm here," Keith said, and kissed Bran on the forehead.

"I love you, Keith."

"I love you too." Keith reached out and turned off the light. Starlight and streetlight shining through the window painted Bran's face silver. They kissed again, a long drawn-out kiss filled with warmth and passion. And Keith felt Bran's hands fumbling at the waist of his jeans.

This is it, Keith thought. Thank you, Frank, at least I know what to do.

In a minute both boys wore just their underpants. They pressed together and Keith dragged the covers up over them. He felt the hot rigidity of Bran pressing against him, matching his own stiffness. Bran's hands played over his back, his thighs, his hips; he nuzzled the older boy and marveled at the silky softness of his skin.

Bran's hands moved beneath the waistband of Keith's shorts, and seconds later the shorts were discarded and Keith was naked next to his friend. While Bran stroked him gently, Keith pulled Bran's shorts off and threw them aside.

So hot…so large, Keith thought, as he moved his hands to Bran's groin. The older boy's fingers drew patterns of fire in Keith's tortured flesh; he moved his own hands and Bran thrust his hips forward, kissed Keith boldly.

"You're so good," Bran whispered. Their hands moved together, in matching, relentless rhythm, and with their free arms the boys embraced, trying to bring their bodies even closer together.

Keith knew that he panted, that he made no coherent noise. He was almost beyond rational thought, when Bran smothered him in a final, demanding kiss. The older boy tensed, and Keith felt himself on the brink of passion's release.

Then, in one glorious moment, it happened. Keith was transported beyond the crisp, clear night, as he and Bran moved together into a plane of joy and bliss far beyond the ordinary world.

Clinging together, overcome by fatigue, the two boys slipped into sleep.

CHAPTER THIRTEEN

Bran and Keith stayed together until late Friday night—and then Saturday afternoon they went Christmas shopping. The big malls were all decorated in poinsettias, holly, and moving figures of Santa and his elves. Although Keith didn't buy anything, he had a wonderful time joking around with Bran, and by the time Bran finally brought him home he was happily exhausted.

Bran stopped the car in front of Keith's house. "All ashore that's going ashore," Bran said.

"You want to come in?"

Bran yawned. "I'd better get home and get some sleep." He ran his fingers through Keith's hair. "Although I'd like nothing better than to come in and try to think of new ways of keeping you awake."

Keith nodded. "Okay. I'm pretty tired too. Talk to you tomorrow?"

"Of course." Bran drew him close, kissed him. "Sleep well."

"You too. Bye."

"Bye."

*

Monday morning Keith found out about two events that showed promise for the future.

The first was the Winter Dance. A poster in the main lobby told Keith that the dance, sponsored by the Student

Government, was to be held on Friday, December 20...the last day of school before winter vacation.

Keith had always liked dances, but at Kinwood he and Frank had never worked up the nerve to go to one together. Maybe Bran would like to go, Keith thought. The idea gave him a warm feeling inside.

The second upcoming event was even more exciting. In drama class Mr. hening announced that Oak Grove would do a trilogy of one-act holiday plays for area elementary schools. "We'll have tryouts Wednesday after school," he said, "And the plays themselves will be presented the week before vacation starts."

"That only gives us two weeks for rehearsal!" a student protested.

Bob Hening smiled. "Isn't that what makes it interesting? I'm going to assign three student directors, and preparation will be quite intensive. This is the sort of experience that will sharpen your acting abilities...you ought to be looking forward to it as a challenge and a great opportunity."

The lunch table crowd was aflutter with the news.

"*I'm* going to apply as director," Debbie said. "An opportunity like this is too good to miss."

"Who do you think the directors are going to be?" Laura asked Bran.

Bran shook his head. "I don't want to say."

"You knew this was going to happen," Warren accused. "Never trust the Drama teacher's aide."

"I didn't know," Bran said. "Okay, you want a guess about directors?" He ticked them off on his fingers. "Debbie, for one. Susan Majors. And Tony Ramierez."

"What about you?" Jane asked.

"No. I directed *Early Frost* in One-Acts last year, remember? That was my sole experience with directing. Never again. Not interested."

Albert leaned back in his chair. "Susan Majors will get her people from the cheerleaders' crowd. Tony Ramierez will pick up Jerry Todd right away, and a couple of the juniors in Student Government. So who among us are going to get parts in the different plays?"

Bran put his fingertips together and looked over them at Bert. "Who indeed? That's the question of the week, isn't it?"

Debbie gave a half-smiled, turned away, and that was the end of the matter for that day.

Bran recruited Keith to help him prepare for the audition. The two boys went to Keith's house, and Bran produced playbooks for the three one-acts that made up the holiday program.

"Where did you get ahold of these?" Keith asked.

"Being drama aide does have its rewards," Bran said. "Bob told me what the plays were going to be, and I borrowed the books from the shelves." Bran put the books down on the kitchen table. "So, which one are you going to try out for?"

"I'm not sure I'm going to try out."

"Nonsense." Bran pointed to the shortest play, a Hanukkah story that featured three male and two female parts. "There's a part in here that's perfect for you."

Keith picked up the book and leafed through it. "What, the old grandfather? Just because I did Mr. Witherspoon doesn't mean that I —"

"No, not the grandfather. The young student. Just out of college, filled with idealism—that's a part you could have fun with, but it wouldn't be too hard."

"Is this the play you're trying out for?"

Bran nodded. "Debbie'll be directing this one, if I know Bob. I'll get the grandfather, you'll be the kid, Warren will get the other male role, and Jane and Laura will do the two females."

"Sounds like it could be fun. I really wasn't thinking about trying out, though."

"Kid, you need to build up your Thespian points. This will be a great experience for you. You can't imagine how intense it is to get a whole play together, start to finish, in two weeks. You'll love it."

Keith nodded. "Okay, you've convinced me. I'll try out."

"Good." Bran took the book and opened it to a particular page. "There's a part here where we have a scene together. If we can learn it before Wednesday night, we'll knock 'em dead at the audition."

*

The directors were indeed as Bran had predicted, and Debbie chose the play he said she would.

By Wednesday morning, Keith felt confident that he and Bran had their parts secured. He knew his lines and Bran had given him enough rough direction that he made a good showing.

By the end of the day stage fright made an unwelcome appearance and Keith was less sure than he had been. Bob Hening sat in the center of the auditorium with the three student directors—together, the four of them would choose the casts for all three plays.

Just before they went on, Bran squeezed Keith's hand affectionately. "Just do as well as you did last night, and we've got the parts."

Shaking, Keith went onstage with Bran. They performed their little scene...Keith was happy and relieved that he remembered his lines and stayed in character. After a shared coke, the two boys went back into the auditorium and sat quietly while others auditioned.

"Thank you," Mr. hening said when it was all over. "We'll have the cast lists posted on the drama room door tomorrow morning. Tony, Susan, Debbie, come with me. The rest of you, go home." His eyes found Bran in the dimness. "Bran, will you close up and then drop the key by the drama room?"

"Sure." Bran took the key from Hening and grinned. "Make good decisions, you three," he said to the student directors.

It didn't take long to clear the auditorium and lock the doors. Bert and Laura joined Bran and Keith in Bran's car. Bert held back and let Keith sit in the front; he got in the back with Laura. They drove around to the drama room and Bran left the engine running. "This'll just take a second," he said, hopping out with Mr. Hening's keys.

When he came back, Laura grabbed him by the arm. "So tell us, what did you hear?"

"They're all four in Bob's office," Bran said, "And when I came in they shut up."

"You didn't hear *anything*?"

"I heard Bob say thank you," Bran offered.

"You're exasperating, Bran Davenport."

"I know." Bran smiled sweetly. "So do you all want to get here early tomorrow?"

There was general agreement.

"Good. Bert, pick you up at seven? Laura, you're next, and Keith about seven-fifteen."

"Seven-fifteen?" Keith moaned. "Do I *have* to?"

They reached a stop sign; Bran leaned over, kissed Keith, and said, "You can make it, kid."

Keith nodded. "Seven-fifteen," he said reluctantly.

*

It was drizzling Thursday morning. Keith was ready when Bran arrived, but he didn't like it.

"You don't look too bright-eyed," Bran said as Keith slid into the front seat.

"I could have really handled another hour in my nice warm bed. It was dry."

"So could we all," Bert responded from the back. "I don't even know why I'm doing this, I didn't even audition for the stupid play."

"Bitch, bitch, bitch," Bran said with a grin. "You're doing this because you're a good friend, that's why."

The school was virtually deserted when they arrived. Bran pulled into the parking lot and skidded to a stop before the drama room. "Everybody out," he said, jumping out of the car.

The cast list was posted on the door. Leaning past Bran, Keith located the list for Debbie's play. And suddenly, he felt as if someone had punched him in the stomach. The two female roles, as Bran had predicted, went to Laura and Jane. But the three male parts were filled by Warren, Rick Lederman, and Steve Meyers, a senior who had not been involved in *Arsenic and Old Lace* at all.

Keith had half-expected that he wouldn't get a part...but he was totally surprised that Bran was not accepted for the production.

Bran stepped back, his face firmly under control. "Congratulations," he said, offering his hand to Laura. "You'll do a fine job."

"I could spit," she answered. "You did ten times better than any of the three of them. Bran, I have a good mind not to take the part."

Bran shook his head. "Don't do that. It's a good part. You'll have fun with it."

"But you...."

Bran shrugged. "What does the Thespian Pledge say? 'I will accept criticisms, disappointments and promotions with humility and obedience.'" He gave a smile, obviously forced. "Hey, you guys go ahead in and save us a table in the Media Center. I'll be along in a little while." Hands in his pockets, Bran walked toward the athletic field.

Laura looked worriedly after him, then at Keith. "Are you okay?"

"Me? Yeah, I'm fine." Keith stared after Bran. "Is he all right?"

"I don't know. Bran's never lost a part like this before. Especially not when he did so well."

"I'll see you guys later, okay?" Keith set off after his friend without waiting for an answer from Laura and Bert.

He caught up with Bran halfway to the athletic field. The sky was grey and white with low clouds, and there was a smell of wet dirt all around. Keith walked quietly next to Bran for a moment, then said, "I'm sorry."

"Yeah, well, it's just something that happens." Bran was quiet...but not the serious quiet that Keith had come to know. This was a quiet as heavy and brooding as the steady cold drizzle.

"You really *did* do better than those guys in tryouts."

Bran stopped, looked at Keith. His damp hair hung down almost in his eyes, and his mouth drooped. "Hey, kid, if you don't mind—let's give the sympathy a rest, okay? I just want to be alone for a few minutes." He touched Keith's face, then withdrew his hand. "Nothing personal. I just need a little time to myself."

Keith shrugged. "Okay, if that's what you want. See you inside?"

"Okay."

Bran trudged on. Keith went back toward school, then turned to see Bran sitting on the bleachers looking out across the athletic field. He sighed.

Leave him alone, he thought, and he'll come home.

Too bad life wasn't as simple as a nursery rhyme....

*

Bran was subdued for the rest of the day. Keith expected some kind of confrontation at lunch, but Debbie said nothing about her choices for actors, and Bran ignored the whole matter. Keith felt that he should be more disappointed at not getting the part, but he was too worried about Bran to spare time for his own feelings.

She didn't give him the part because of me, he thought in the middle of history class. She wanted to hurt him because she thinks he's chosen me over her. And so she picked other people for the play.

He's unhappy, and I'm responsible.

That night Keith called Bran. The call wasn't very satisfactory—after a few minutes Bran said that he had to take a shower. "Oh," said Keith, "all right. I guess I'll see you in school tomorrow."

"Guess so," Bran said. "Good night."

Keith set the phone back in its cradle and frowned. He wanted to talk to his mother, but he wasn't sure what to tell her. So he shrugged and decided to wait until the next day. After a few inadequate chapters of his latest mystery novel, he turned off the light and went to sleep.

Bran didn't show up between classes the next day. It wasn't until lunchtime that Keith found out that the older boy hadn't come to school at all.

"Is he sick?" he asked.

Bert shrugged. "I don't know. I talked to him last night, he sounded okay to me. Maybe he had car trouble."

"Maybe," Keith said.

As soon as he got home, he called Bran's number. Bran's father answered.

"Hello, may I speak with Bran?"

"He can't come to the phone right now."

"Oh," Keith said, stupidly. "Well, could you tell him that Keith called?"

"Right." Without waiting for more, Bran's father hung up.

Keith frowned. I don't believe I like that man, he thought.

Keith ate dinner, watched television, and did his homework all with one eye on the clock. Finally, at eleven-thirty, he decided it was too late for Bran to call him, and he went to bed. Tomorrow, he thought, I will find out what is going on.

Saturday morning, after the Bugs Bunny/Road Runner show, Keith called Bran's house. Again Mr. Davenport answered.

"Hello, this is Keith Graff. Is Bran home."

"He's home, but he's sleeping."

"Do you have any idea when he'll be up?"

"Can't say. This cold really has him worn out."

"Oh, okay. I guess I'll just wait for him to call me."

"Fine."

"Goodbye," Keith said, but it was too late. He spoke to a dead line.

By evening Keith was a quivering bundle of nerves. The weather didn't make things any easier—it was raining steadily, so he couldn't hop on his bike and run over to Bran's for a sympathy visit. And his mother used the car all day for shopping, so he was stranded.

At quarter of seven the phone rang, and he pounced on it.

"Hello?"

"Keith, this is Laura."

"Oh. Hi."

"Do you know what's going on with Bran?"

"No. I've called a couple of times, and his father told me he had a cold."

"Same story here. But I just called Debbie's, and they told me she went to see Bran."

"Great," Keith said sarcastically. "That's all he needs."

"Are you free?"

"Sure. Why?"

"How about if I come over and pick you up, and then we can swing by Bran's house. We can say that we were in the neighborhood and we decided to drop by." She chuckled. "Got any chicken soup?"

"Chicken soup?"

"Yeah, you know, chicken soup. The stuff you give people with colds. If you have a can, bring it. It'll be a good peace offering."

Fifteen minutes later, armed with cans of chicken noodle soup, Keith and Laura pulled up in front of Bran's house. Debbie's car was parked next to the driveway.

"What do we do?" Laura said.

"I don't suppose we can just walk up and knock on the door?"

"Might as well give it a try."

When they were halfway up the front walk, the door opened and Debbie appeared, pulling on her coat. "Well, well, what are you two doing here?"

Keith held up his can of chicken soup. "Bran's sick—we thought we'd make a sympathy visit."

Debbie nodded. "Sweet idea." She looked at Laura. "Bran's *very* sick. He's sleeping right now, and I know he doesn't want to see anybody." She walked away from the house, took her car keys from a pocket. "As a matter of fact, he just threw me out a few minutes ago. I've been talking to his father."

What's going on here? Keith thought. She doesn't want me to see him. Why? Jealousy?

"When do you suppose we could visit him? Tomorrow?"

Debbie pursed her lips. "Probably not. He's got the flu something terrible. And he's probably contagious." She shivered. "Don't worry, I'll take good care of him."

From the way she faintly stressed "I'll," Keith knew that jealousy was indeed the problem.

"Oh, well," Laura said, "I'll give him a call tomorrow and see how he's feeling. At least he should know that *all* his friends care about him." She turned abruptly and went to her car; Keith nodded goodbye to Debbie and followed.

"Who does she think she is?" Laura said as they pulled away. "Telling us that we can't see Bran!"

"It's me," Keith said, looking down. "She doesn't want to let me in to see him. I think she's said something to Bran's father, too."

"I don't see what Debbie's problem is. All day in rehearsal yesterday, she kept talking about Bran. And saying bad things about you."

"Like what?" The news didn't surprise Keith; he just wished it could be different. Debbie had been a good friend, he thought, before all this started with Bran.

"She calls you a wimp. She said that you have all the sensitivity of…let me get this right…an orange peel. She thinks Bran would be better off with someone like her."

"Of course she does."

"Damn," Laura said, pounding her fist on the steering wheel. "We're going to get you in to see Bran, Keith. If Debbie's been talking to him, she's probably telling him all the things she was telling us."

"Great. That's all I need. At least I can trust Bran to make up his own mind, and not pay attention to what she says."

"I'm not so sure about that. Bran can be pretty stupid where Debbie is concerned. He just doesn't realize that she has a mean streak way down inside her."

"So what are we going to do?"

"Bran's father goes to church with the Vovcenkos every Sunday morning—he used to go to the eleven o'clock service and then spend some time over at Debbie's. I remember, because I've been there sometimes when they came home." She took a breath. "So here's what you do. Get over to Bran's tomorrow about ten-thirty, and as soon as Mr. Davenport leaves, make your move."

"And what if Debbie's there, taking care of him?"

Laura grinned. "I'll see that she isn't. I'll drop by her house about nine-thirty and tell her it's time to work on our history project. I'll keep her busy, don't worry."

On impulse, Keith leaned over and kissed Laura on the cheek. "Thanks, Laura. You don't know how much this means."

"I think I do," she said.

CHAPTER FOURTEEN

It had stopped raining Sunday morning. The streets were still wet, and crystal drops fell from the overhanging branches of trees as Keith pedaled past. There was a dry wind from the south, and the sun was out for the first time in days.

It took Keith only fifteen minutes to bike to Bran's house; he arrived about ten-fifteen and parked his bike by a fire hydrant across the street while he watched the house. Shortly before ten-thirty Bran's father left. Keith smiled when he saw that his mental image of the man was right in every detail, down to the wide shoulders, paunchy stomach, and dark hair thinning on top. Mr. Davenport got into his car and drove away; as soon as he was off the street Keith wheeled his bike up to Bran's house and left it parked in the driveway.

Hesitantly, Keith knocked on the door—five quick taps. He counted to twenty, then knocked again.

The lock turned, the door opened, and he faced Bran.

The older boy wore a pair of blue pajamas that were a size too big, and a frayed terrycloth bathrobe without a belt. His hair was uncombed, his eyes were red, and he looked pale. But when he saw that it was Keith, he smiled. "Come on in."

Bran's living room was done in plush beige carpet, comfortable green chairs, and a large sofa that was now fixed up as a sickbed. On the coffee table was a box of tissues, cough syrup and aspirin, a glass of orange juice, and a paperback science-fiction novel with a reddish-brown cover featuring spaceships and a king on a throne. A large television with accompanying video recorder was dark in the corner.

Bran took off his robe, settled on the couch, and pulled an afghan over himself. "Sit down," he said, and Keith sat facing him.

"How are you feeling?"

Bran grinned weakly. "Awful."

"I missed you when you weren't in school."

"Yeah, well..." Bran gestured around himself, "I couldn't make it."

"I called—your father said you were sleeping."

Bran frowned. "Dad didn't say anything about you calling. Just Debbie." He sighed. "I was beginning to think nobody loved me."

"*I* love you."

Bran looked up at him with a sad face. "Hey, you didn't really have to come visit. I mean, I might be contagious or something."

"Oh, are *you* trying to get rid of me, too?"

"What do you mean by that? Who's been trying to get rid of you?"

"When Laura and I stopped by last night, we got the feeling that Debbie was trying to keep us away from you."

Bran closed his eyes. "You're being paranoid. Debbie said that you guys drove by, but when she told you I was sleeping you said you didn't want to bother me."

"When did she tell you all this?"

"Last night. After you guys left."

"I thought she was going home."

Bran shook his head. "No. She stayed here until about ten last night. We talked a lot."

Keith felt confused. "Wait a minute. That's not the impression Debbie gave me." He sighed. "Well, I'm here now, that's the important thing. Do you think you'll be able to come to school tomorrow?"

"I don't know. I'm still feeling pretty bad."

"Poor boy." Keith leaned over and put his hand on the older boy's forehead. "At least you don't have a fever." He moved his hand, tenderly stroked Bran's unshaven chin.

Bran reached up and stopped him. "Don't," he said, looking away.

A nervousness as intense as stage fright hit Keith. "What's wrong?"

"Nothing."

For a second Keith was ready to accept that. Then a feeling very much like anger flared within him. "Don't tell me *Nothing*. Something's bothering you. Is it the play? Bran, you can't let yourself get upset because you lost a part —"

"It's not the play."

"What, then?"

"Keith…I think we might be going too fast. You and me."

"Too fast?"

"Falling in love and all that. It's happening too quickly."

Keith swallowed. "O-okay. Let's talk about it. Do you think we should…should stop seeing one another?"

Bran looked pained. "No. I…look, kid, I love you. But there are things we haven't figured on."

Keith sat down on the floor and looked at Bran, face-to-face. "Like what? Tell me, and we'll talk about them."

For a while Bran was silent, looking into Keith's eyes.

Keith forced a laugh. "It can't be that bad, can it?"

"Kid, I love you. But I just don't know if I love you enough to…to give up my friends."

"Who's asking you to?"

Again Bran looked as if he were suffering from a stomach ache. "Nobody's asking me. I'm not blind, though, I can see what's going on. Debbie talking to me last night made a lot of things clear. I can't control personalities, and I can't help it if two people I like don't like each other. But if it keeps on like this the whole gang is going to split up. This is just what I was afraid of with Warren."

Keith didn't know what to say. He thought for a moment, then, "You mean Debbie and me. She's jealous, Bran."

"I can see that. She's also persuasive. She's got Warren convinced, I don't know, that you're seducing me or something like that—so Warren isn't too fond of you right now. And I think Debbie's going to win Jane and Rick over to her side."

"And that's why you didn't get the part. I thought so."

"That doesn't have anything to do with it." Bran coughed and took a drink of orange juice. "Okay, maybe it does. The whole point is, I don't like this stuff of people taking sides. The whole gang is in danger of breaking up."

"Because of me."

"*No.* Because of me." He hung his head. "I should have waited until this year was over."

Keith stood up. "So what do you want me to do?" He felt very close to crying, and he tried to cover his feelings by getting mad. "Do you want me to just walk out of here and not see you again, so that I won't be breaking up the gang?" He took a ragged breath. "It's not my fault, and I can't do anything to stop it, but if they mean that much to you I'll leave."

"Don't do this to me, Keith."

"Don't do this to you? To *you*?! What about me? I...I love you, Bran. I love you more than I've ever loved anybody else... my mother, Frank, anybody. There's nothing I wouldn't do for you. Even..." his words caught in his throat, sharp jagged corners. "Even leaving you alone. If you make me."

"Look, maybe you're a little young to —"

Keith stamped his foot. "I'm only a year younger than you are!" Now he *was* crying, and he didn't care. "So maybe I'm new to this school, and maybe I haven't had all the experience that you people have—but I'm not a little kid. Damn it, I'm nearly seventeen, I think I'm just as ready as you are to fall in love."

"Okay," Bran said, raising his voice, "Maybe neither of us is ready. Maybe we *ought* to cool things down a little while we think about this. Maybe there is a way to reconcile the gang. If we take some time, we can find it."

"And if not? I guess we'll just call it quits, then?"

"Keith, don't do this to me. Don't make me choose between you and my friends."

"I'm not the one making you choose."

"I have to choose anyway."

"Fine!" Keith snatched up his coat, went to the door. "Go ahead and choose. Do whatever you want. I don't care." He left the house, slammed the door behind him. All the way home he fumed.

Mom was not in—she had gone on a sightseeing trip with people from her office. Keith blundered into the house, went upstairs, and fell on his bed for a good, long cry.

*

Monday was miserable.

A cold front moved through the area Sunday night, so that Monday's weather was chilly and still damp from the long rain. Waiting for the bus, Keith told himself that it was only to be expected—this was, after all, the second week of December —yet still he wished it could be warm.

Bad enough that I have to feel lousy, h thought, without being cold as well.

After arriving at school he went right to his physics classroom and read the next chapter before school started. After Drama class he deliberately didn't wait by the door… Frau Schneider raised her eyebrows when he was early for German for the first time in months. He didn't know if Bran was in today; all he knew was that he couldn't face his friend after the fight Sunday.

At lunchtime he intentionally sat far across the cafeteria. It was like a replay of his first weeks at Oak Grove: he sat by himself and ate his sandwich and apple while staring off unhappily into space.

He did notice that Bran wasn't at the usual table. If he wasn't staying home with his sickness, he was avoiding Keith the same way Keith was avoiding him.

Let him, Keith thought. I'm not the one who decided that he has to choose between me and them.

Just the same, his lunch didn't have much taste, and he felt as if tears were waiting to stream from his eyes.

He spent Monday night reading and watching television. His mother, busy with the laundry, had little attention to spare for him.

Tuesday was nearly the same up until lunch. As Keith sat alone in self-imposed exile, he saw that Bran was back, apparently as noisy and cheerful as ever. Keith turned away and concentrated on his sandwich as much as he could.

When he looked up, Laura was standing next to him. "Mind if I sit down?" she said.

Keith shrugged. "Go ahead."

She sat next to him, looked him right in the eyes. "Do you want to tell me what's wrong?"

"Nothing's wrong. Everything's fine."

"Come on, Keith. Is it something I did?"

"Of course not. It's nothing anybody did. I just...decided that I want to be alone for a while. I need time to myself."

She cocked her head. "I get the feeling that that's not true."

He shrugged again.

"Look at me. Won't you tell me what's wrong? Is it something between you and Bran?"

"Don't worry about it," Keith said bitterly. "It's just a phase I'm going through. I admit I have a lot more growing up to do, okay? I just have to do it at my own pace. Can't everybody just leave me alone?"

Laura drew back. "What brought *that* on?"

"Look, I know everybody thinks I'm immature. I'm not arguing the point."

Laura frowned. "Who told you that? Bran? I can't believe it, Bran Davenport telling someone *else* that they're immature. Bran Davenport, the expert on maturity."

Keith faced Laura as calmly as he could. "Listen, I had a talk with Bran. He says that having me around it just wrecking your gang. So I've decided to do the decent thing and bow out, okay? Keep the gang together."

"And I can't believe I'm hearing you say this. Do you have some idea that we've all been tolerating you for Bran's sake? That's not the case. You're a good friend, Keith, and I hoped you could stay that way." She stopped, looked back at the communal lunch table. "It's Debbie, isn't it?"

"Debbie, and Warren, and Jane and Rick, from what I was told. And probably half the rest of the school."

Laura tightened her lips. "Listen to me, Keith Graff. Nobody—not Debbie, not Bran, not anybody else—tells me who I can be friends with. So Debbie's got Bran convinced that the gang will break up if he keeps seeing you...I'll go back there and do a little convincing of my own. As far as I'm concerned, if you're not part of it then there isn't any gang."

Keith closed his eyes and sighed heavily. "Don't do that, Laura. I-I just want Bran to be happy. If you go back there and start making all kinds of ultimatums, then he's going to be unhappy. It won't help things. I've thought it over, and this is the best way. I'm going to stay away from now on."

"He's got you brainwashed pretty well, doesn't he? What about *your* happiness? Doesn't that count for anything?"

"I know what I'm doing. Please."

Laura shook her head. "I don't understand you at all."

"Just do me a favor. Promise you won't issue ultimatums?"

"Is that what you want?"

"Yes."

"Okay," she conceded. "I promise. But I still think it's wrong."

"Thanks. Now go back and make sure Bran's okay. If…if he asks, tell him that I'm not going to cause trouble for him."

"I'm not going to give you up, Keith."

"Please?"

Laura nodded, and went back to the group table. A few minutes later the bell rang, and Keith trudged to history class with a heavy heart.

*

Finally, he had to call Frank.

Luckily, his friend answered right away. "Good to hear from you, fella. How are things going?"

"Bad, Frank. Real bad."

"What's up?" Frank said, his voice instantly serious and compassionate.

"Bran and I had a fight. A bad one." Keith explained what had happened Sunday, and the events that led up to it. Frank listened patiently. "So what am I going to do?" Keith asked.

"Depends."

"On what?"

"On how much you need him—and how much he needs *you*."

"What do you mean?"

"If you decide that you can't stand to be without him, then you go crawling back to him and tell him that you were wrong. Then talk to him about how the two of you can live with his friends, and hopefully everything will get straightened out. I doubt it, though. That Debbie sounds like she has it out for you, and she's going to do the best she can to break the two of you up."

"What else can I do? I mean, other than going on like I am now. I can't do this forever."

"There's another alternative. Hold tight, don't do anything. Another day or two, and Bran decides he can't live without you, he comes crawling to you and apologizes."

"I don't know if he'll do that."

Frank was silent for a minute. "Don't underestimate yourself, Keith. You're a good fella. If I was Bran, and you were in love with me, I would do a little extra to keep you."

"I don't think it's likely, Frank."

"Do me a favor, then? Since you don't have anything to lose—wait two more days. If you haven't heard from him by Thursday night, then Friday morning you apologize to him and take your lumps."

Keith sighed. "Even apologizing to him isn't going to change the basic situation. He still has to choose between me and them."

"Maybe he does. Keith, you're trying to make his choice for him. They're *his* friend."

"Some of them are mine, too."

"Not the ones who are causing the problem. Keith, boy, do you trust Bran? Do you think he's a good person?"

"Yes." Keith didn't even have to think about his answer. Even if they had fought—Bran was still a good person.

"Then take my word for it, he's as upset about hurting you as you are about hurting him. And he's probably on the phone with his friends right now, taking advice on how to get you back."

"Sorry, Frank, I just don't think you're right."

"But you'll wait until Thursday night, won't you?"

"It's silly."

"Do it for my sake," Frank said with great intensity.

Keith shrugged. "All right, I'll wait until Thursday night."

"And call me Thursday, whether you hear from him or not?"

"I'll call you."

"Good. Now go to sleep and don't worry about anything."

"Okay. I'll talk to you later."

"Goodnight, Keith. I love you."

Keith forced a smile. "I love you too. Goodnight."

"And Keith —"

"Yes?"

"You'd better be there when I start having *my* first love affair. If I'm going to screw it up as badly as you are, I'm going to need all the help I can get."

Keith gave a genuine smile. "I'll be there. Go to sleep."

Thursday.

How could he live until then?

CHAPTER FIFTEEN

"Keith, you're not paying attention."

"Huh? Oh, I'm sorry, Mom." Keith ate another spoonful of oatmeal—growing cold now—and looked up at his mother. "What were you saying?"

"I'm thinking of going out of town this weekend. Is it all right if I leave you alone here?"

"Out of town? With Mr. Stamler, I guess?" For a few weeks now Keith's mother had been dating a man she met at work.

"As a matter of fact, yes. Pete got tickets to that hot new show on Broadway, and he wants to make it a long weekend in New York. Sort of to celebrate finishing up the new account."

Keith shrugged his shoulders. "It's fine with me. It's about time you had a vacation...you spent all your leave time this summer settling the house and getting ready for the move."

"Will you be all right?"

"I'll be fine."

"If you want to have someone over to keep you company, you can."

"Thanks. But that doesn't look likely right now. Never mind, I'll have a good time anyway. When will you leave?"

"We're going to call the travel agent today. We'll probably take off Friday morning and not come back until Tuesday or Wednesday."

Keith finished up is oatmeal and put his bowl in the sink. "Sounds great. Do you think you can pack in just two days?" It was an old family joke, that Keith's mother was the world's worst packer.

"No problem, smarty." She looked at the clock, then sat down. "Keith...is everything okay? You've been dragging lately, and what with the new account I've been too busy to give you much attention."

"Things haven't been going too well. Bran and I had a fight." He forced a smile. "But it'll be over with any day now. It's just a matter of who apologizes first."

She looked him in the eyes. "My little boy is growing up. Can I be silly and give you a piece of motherly advice?"

"Of course."

"I may not know everything there is to know about relationships...I certainly didn't manage too well with your father. But there's one thing *my* mother told me, that I've never forgotten." She paused, then said, "Never let the sun go down on your anger. If you're mad at someone, be sure that you make up before the day is out. Regardless of who has to apologize, or whose pride gets hurt. Make sure you talk things out and settle the matter. Otherwise it can build and build, and soon you'll find that you won't have any way out at all." She looked off into space, then shook her head. "Like I say, it's silly motherly advice. You don't have to take it. I know *I* didn't."

I have the best mother in the world, Keith thought for the thousandth time in the last few months. "Thanks, Mom. It's good to know that you care."

All during the long, cold wait for the bus, and then the ride to school, Keith thought about what his mom had said. he thought about his promise to Frank. Here it was only Wednesday—he had told Frank he would wait until Friday before apologizing to Bran.

Suppose Mom was right?

Then enough damage was done already, he decided. Another two days wouldn't cause any more trouble.

He hoped.

Keith made his now-customary appearance in German class just a few minutes after Drama, not waiting for Bran at all. In algebra, Jane kept quiet, as she had done all week— Keith didn't know what she was thinking, and didn't want to guess. At lunch he took his place at his own table, and did his best to pay no attention to Bran's table.

He was only halfway through his sandwich, when he felt someone creep up behind him, and turned to see a somewhat abashed Bran.

The older boy smiled and threw back his shoulders. "Ah, Prince Trueheart, I presume?"

"Cut it out, Bran."

"Your Highness, I have traveled the breadth of the kingdom to see you. I have slain the evil dragon. I have battled the evil wizard who enchanted this castle. I swam the moat. Twice. I have made my way through the unspeakable horrors of the dungeons and won my way to your side. Pray do not refuse to hear me now. I love you, Prince, and I repent the things I said that drove you forth. Accept, please, my humble apologies."

"Bran, what are you doing?"

"I'm apologizing to you, you little twit. Don't spoil my scene. Do you want me on my knees? Okay." Bran dropped to his knees and took Keith's hand. "Keith, I love you and I'm sorry I hurt you. I can't stand it without you, and I want you to come back to me. There, does that make it clear?"

"Oh, Bran." Keith lowered his head, mostly to hide the tears that were gathering in his eyes.

"Forgive me?"

"I…of course I forgive you. Stand up."

They both stood. Keith looked into Bran's face for a second, then Bran hugged him tightly. "I love you so much."

It wasn't the time or place, but Keith had to know. "What about choosing between me and your friends?"

"I don't have to choose. I'll make that clear to everyone." Bran patted him on the back. "Don't ever leave me again, you hear? Especially when I've got the plague—I almost died."

"Don't ever give me the opportunity. I was scared."

"You're back now, and that's what counts." They walked back to the gang's table. Laura, smiling, trotted up with Keith's books and the rest of his lunch.

Debbie leaned back in her chair and clasped her hands. "Well, well," she said derisively, "The prodigal son returns. I thought we'd seen the last of you."

Bran took Keith's hand and faced Debbie. "We're going to have this out here and now. Keith is my friend, and from here on we are a team. Where I go, he goes...so if you want me, you're going to have to like him."

Debbie raised her nose. "Why are you telling *me* this? I've been perfectly polite to him. Keith, even you have to admit that I'm right."

"Sure you've been polite," Bran said, not giving Keith a chance to answer. "And behind his back you're saying nasty stuff. I want that stopped right now."

"Bran, it's none of my business who you date. But you don't have the right to ask the rest of us to socialize with him. He's...."

"Yes?"

"He's just not our type of person."

Keith felt like an animal being inspected for butchering.

"You liked him well enough before I started going with him. You know you did."

"That was different."

Laura stared at Debbie. "Come on, Deb. Admit that you're jealous of Keith and get it over with. Then we can all kiss and make up."

Debbie took Warren's hand. "It doesn't matter if I was jealous. I certainly don't have any reason to be jealous now."

"No, you don't," Bert said, quietly. "So give it up. Debbie, *everybody* gets jealous at some time, it's nothing to be ashamed of. Can't you just forgive Keith, forgive yourself, and let things drop?"

There was a long moment of silence, while Keith felt as if he were waiting to walk out on stage and start a play. Then Debbie lowered her eyes.

"Keith," she said slowly and deliberately, "I am sorry I mistreated you. You are welcome to stay at our lunch table… and be our friend."

Keith thought it was time to be magnanimous. "Hey, Debbie, I don't blame you for what you did. You were just looking out for Bran."

"Group hug!" Laura shouted, and the whole gang joined in a massive hug.

Everything was as it should be, Keith thought.

Then, across the circle, Debbie's eyes met his, and in her gaze he read a lingering hostility.

It wasn't over yet….

*

After school Bran drove Keith home, then came in to eat some cookies and talk. Keith didn't allow their conversation to get too heavy…he was afraid of provoking another argument, and that was the last thing they wanted.

When both boys had eaten enough cookies, they adjourned to the couch. Bran sat down sideways and Keith rested his back against Bran's chest while Bran wrapped his arms around the younger boy. Hand to hand and cheek to cheek, they talked gently about school, the weather, Christmas, and whatever other subjects popped into their minds.

"Are you busy this weekend?" Keith asked suddenly.

"I don't think so. Why?"

"Mom's gonna be away, and she said I could have a friend over to keep me company."

Bran squeezed Keith and smiled. "Fun and games all weekend. Sounds wonderful."

"I didn't say I was inviting you. I might ask Laura over."

"Creep." Bran tickled him, and Keith squirmed, laughing.

"Okay, okay, you're invited! Stop tickling me."

"I'd love to come over."

"What about your father?"

"What about him?"

"Call me paranoid, but I get the feeling he doesn't approve of me."

"You know how it is. Fathers never approve of anybody you go out with. Dad doesn't own me—and he knows that. I keep my mouth shut about his life, and he does the same for me."

"Good. Why don't you come over after school on Friday, then? Mom said no wild parties, but we can probably have the gang over if you want."

Bran hugged him. "Or we could just stay home together." He turned his head, and kissed Keith.

Keith twisted, put his arms around Bran, and in another minute they were kissing passionately. Keith ran his hands over Bran's body, rubbed his shoulders and back as he drove his tongue deep into Bran's welcoming mouth.

A while later Bran pulled back slightly. "Mmm. Hey, kid, we'd better stop this or we're going to shock your mother when she comes home."

"You're right...I'd forgotten that she was coming back." Keith looked at his watch. "I hate to throw you out, but I'm supposed to vacuum before Mom gets home, and—"

"Yeah, I have chores to do too." Bran stood up, retrieved his coat from the rack, and hugged Keith. "See you tomorrow," he said, with a quick goodbye kiss.

Keith smiled, and went to get the vacuum cleaner.

*

Friday after school Bran drove home with Keith. He took his overnight bag out of the trunk, and carried his things upstairs to Keith's room just as if he belonged.

He *does* belong here, Keith thought. At least, if *I* have anything to do with it.

"What's first on the agenda?" Bran asked, sitting down at the kitchen table.

"Homework, I guess," Keith answered. "It's Friday, let's get it out of the way."

"Fine with me."

The two boys worked at the kitchen table. It gave Keith a secure feeling to look up every so often and meet Bran's eyes over a book, or just to see that his friend was there.

Love is supposed to be fireworks and explosions, he thought. And sometimes it is. But nobody ever tells you about these moments, just being with him and knowing that he's there. The way he chews on his pencil while he's reading, the little flip of his hand to straighten his hair—those are the things I love.

When Keith finished his homework he sat for a few minutes, contentedly watching Bran. Eventually Bran closed his book and looked up, smiling. "What are you doing?"

"Watching you."

Bran rested his chin in his right hand, tilting his head a bit. "Watching me, huh?"

"You're beautiful, you know that?"

"Flattery will get you everywhere." Bran stretched. "But dinner would be nice, too, you know. Wow, it's almost six."

Keith looked at his watch. "I didn't realize. Sure, we ought to make dinner. Mom left something out of the freezer." He peered into the refrigerator. "How does fried chicken strike you?"

"Sounds great. We can have mashed potatoes too."

"I don't know how to make them," Keith confessed.

"I do. It's a lot like scrambled eggs, really."

"Go on." Keith giggled at the mental image of breaking open a potato and scrambling it in a frying pan.

"Okay, so it's not like scrambled eggs. It's still fun. Give me the potatoes, you take the chicken, and we'll see who gets done first."

Keith worked quickly but carefully, as his mother had taught him...especially when it came time to turn the battered chicken in its hot grease. As he worked, Bran was a constant presence at his side or back. A few times, when the older boy was reaching for utensils or when Keith was using the sink, they touched—once or twice Bran took the opportunity to steal a brief kiss.

By the time dinner was ready, Keith felt very warm inside.

If only it could be this way all the time, he thought.

It *could*. In the future.

After dinner the boys consigned the dishes to the dishwasher, and settled on the couch to watch TV. When Keith yawned, Bran beckoned him and he laid down, resting his head in the older boy's lap.

"You're pretty beautiful yourself," Bran said, running his fingers gently through Keith's hair. Softly, Bran moved his fingers over Keith's face, tracing eyebrows and cheekbones— Keith reached up and did the same, then let his hands linger at Bran's neck and shoulders.

Almost without conscious design, the boys kissed—slow, lazy, and sensual.

"This is where we left off the other afternoon," Bran said.

"Yeah, but this time Mom isn't coming home soon," Keith murmured, turning on his side and wrapping one arm around Bran.

For a while they hugged and wrestled a bit, and kissed a little more. Then Keith, uncomfortable, turned—and both boys suddenly fell to the floor, laughing.

Bran gave him a little tickle. "This couch just isn't big enough, kid."

"So why are we still down here?" Keith turned off the TV and sent Bran scurrying upstairs. He walked around the house, made sure all the lights were off and the doors locked, and then followed.

Bran was waiting for him just inside the bedroom door. For a long while the two of them stood in the middle of the floor, embracing and kissing—then Bran laid down on the bed and pulled Keith down next to him.

Again they kissed, and as they did Bran rolled on top of Keith and held him pinned against the mattress. Keith didn't struggle as Bran took off his shirt, then kissed his chest with slow, tantalizing movements of his lips and tongue. Bran's hands on his body brought him to a state of almost painful arousal; when Bran doffed his own shirt Keith reached hungrily for his bare torso, ran his hands over Bran's smooth skin and marveled that someone as wonderful as Bran could love him.

In another minute, Bran loosened Keith's jeans and pulled them off, leaving Keith unclothed on the bed. Bran kissed him on the lips, still holding him down—a kiss that was demanding and aflame with passion. Their bodies pressed together, and Bran moved his hands over Keith's chest, teased his sensitive nipples, touched his thighs, kneaded his buttocks. Keith moaned.

Then Bran kissed each of Keith's nipples in turn, moved down further, gave full attention to the younger boy's navel and his flat stomach. His powerful arms braced against Keith's chest and shoulders still held him down.

Then Keith gasped, as he felt the warmth and wetness of Bran's mouth close over his engorged flesh. He had never known anything like this, had never dreamed of it...!

He struggled, but Bran was too strong for him, and after a long moment he slumped against the bed, weak with passion. He could do nothing as Bran continued his task, nothing but groan incoherently and close his eyes. Soon it was too much for him—he gritted his teeth, and when the instant of release arrived he felt he would pass out.

"Oh, God, Bran, that was..." words failed him, and he could only hug Bran with all his strength. Gingerly, Keith parted Bran's trousers, slid them over the boy's hips, and bowed his head.

"Hey, kid, you don't have to...."

Keith looked up, met Bran's eyes. "I *want* to." If I can make him feel as good as he made me feel....

Later, tired but happy, Keith clung to Bran and drifted between sleep and wakefulness. Bran nuzzled him,, then gave him a sleepy kiss...then the older boy's breathing became slow and deep, and Keith smiled.

This is all I want in the world, he thought. If I can have him, I'm happy.

He closed his eyes.

CHAPTER SIXTEEN

"Good morning."

Keith woke to the aroma of coffee and bacon. He stretched, smiled, opened his eyes—and sat up with a start. Bran, in his pajamas, stood holding a tray laden with bacon, eggs, toast, and coffee.

"Slide over." Bran sat the tray down on the nightstand and crawled into bed with Keith. Bran kissed him and handed him a cup of coffee.

"Gee, this is the first time I've ever had breakfast in bed. How long have you been up?"

"About an hour. It took a while to find things in the kitchen. I hope you like your eggs scrambled."

"Love 'em." Keith kissed Bran, then both boys fell to the task of eating.

Bran's body was warm next to Keith's, the food good. When they were finished, Keith snuggled against Bran and rubbed his face against the slightly fuzzy material of his pajama top.

"I wish we could stay like this all day," he said lazily.

"Why not? What have we got to do today?"

"The dishes."

"They'll wait." Bran pulled the covers up further, tucking them around Keith's exposed shoulder. This was how Keith wanted to wake up every morning…with Bran next to him, holding him.

The boys wound up making love: slowly, deliberately, and with an intensity that surprised Keith. I'm just learning, he thought, what love is—and if I had any sense at all, I would be scared that it's too much.

We've had one fight, and it nearly killed me. Is Mom right —am I foolish to get this attached to him?

And if I am? Will I stop loving him, here and now?

No. Whatever the future brings…I love Bran, and that's all there is to it.

"I almost forgot," Keith said. "Can we go to the Winter Dance next Friday?"

"What, together? I'd like that."

"Good." Keith smiled. "It's a date, then."

The boys spent just about every minute of the weekend together—showering, eating, shopping, or just sitting on the couch reading. Keith had a taste of what it was like to live with someone, the way married couples lived together—and he found that he liked it.

Monday morning Keith made breakfast, and the two boys went to school together. They were almost late—they'd spent too much time snuggling that morning. Together they raced into the building, then Bran gave Keith a hasty kiss and they separated to go to their first classes.

After Keith's Drama class Bran showed up almost at once. The two boys stood outside the door, hand in hand, and before Keith had to leave he took a minute to kiss Bran.

Tony Ramierez, the Student Government leader, pushed past the boys with disdain. "Don't you guys think you're going beyond the bounds of decency?"

Keith pulled back, but Bran held onto his hands as he faced Tony. "Not really. I've seen you and Susan Majors doing the same sort of thing."

"At least Susan and I are discreet. We don't stand in the doorway blocking traffic."

Bran squeezed Keith's hand, nodded. "You'd better get to class. I'll see you at lunch, kid." He turned back to Tony and the two went into the Drama room.

Keith went on to German, disturbed. Why couldn't people mind their own business? First Debbie causing all the trouble, and now Tony Ramierez...would he and Bran never have any peace?

Why couldn't people see that Keith and Bran were happy, and be happy themselves?

Keith shook his head, and opened his German book.

*

Monday night Keith and Bran decorated the house for Christmas. Keith knew where all the boxes were, and while they worked they talked about past Christmases, family traditions, and favorite presents both received and given. When Keith found a few sprigs of plastic mistletoe, he held one up and Bran kissed him under it. One thing led to another, and soon they were making love again.

"Mom's coming home tomorrow," Keith said later.

"I know. I guess my father'll be glad to see me...but I'm sure going to miss you."

"Maybe this summer we can go on vacation somewhere together. I don't know, maybe I can convince Mom to take a week at the beach."

"That sounds good." Bran kissed him.

And after this summer, when Bran went away to college?

Keith shrugged. he would deal with that when it happened.

At lunchtime Tuesday the matter of the Winter Dance came up, and Bran announced that he and Keith were going together.

Debbie frowned, opened her mouth, then closed it.

"What, Debbie?" Bran said.

"Nothing. It's none of my business."

"Go on, say whatever you're thinking of. I don't want any more hidden resentments. From now on, when we have problems we're going to talk them out and get them settled."

Debbie sighed. "I just can't believe that you two are going to the dance together. Bran, you're already the laughingstock of the school...behaving like the hero of some silly romance novel. And Keith's worse. Can't you guys keep that sort of thing at home where it belongs?"

Bran took a breath. "I've been the laughingstock of the school most of my life, Debbie, for one thing and another. Being in Drama. The way I play soccer. Wearing Halloween costumes to school. It doesn't bother me this time."

"But it bothers the rest of us. Bran, it used to mean something to be part of the Thespians. But lately it seems like you're giving all of us a bad name."

Laura snorted. "That's enough, Deb."

Bran held up a hand. "No, it's not enough. Is what she's saying right?" He looked around the table for confirmation.

Warren cleared his throat. "You've got to admit, Bran, that people seem to be avoiding us more than ever lately. Susan Majors said that she's not going to have anything to do with Drama after she finishes her holiday play. Tony Ramierez..."

"Yes, I know Tony's views."

Jane leaned back in her chair. "I don't want to tell you guys what to do...but I think it would be best if you don't go to the dance together."

Bran looked exasperated. "I can't believe this!"

Debbie folded her arms. "Bran, you're a very popular person. At least, you used to be. Then Keith came along, and...."

Keith frowned. "It keeps coming back to me. What's the trouble?"

Debbie snorted, and Jane looked compassionate. "I'm just telling you what people say, Keith: You're new, that's one thing. Oak Grove has a lot of cliques, and you really don't fit into any of them. And you're a junior—but you hang around with seniors all the time. And...okay, except for us, you haven't really gone out of your way to make friends. A lot of people say you're stuck up." She sighed. "And then there's the fact that you're going with Bran. There are more than a few people jealous of you for that." She glanced at Debbie, then away. "Those are all things that will pass...but meanwhile, you've got to understand that you aren't exactly the most popular person at this school."

"And because of that," Bran said, "I'm supposed to stop seeing Keith? Throw him to the wolves?"

"Nobody said you had to stop seeing him. Just—quit doing it so much. And so obviously."

"Or else?"

Debbie shrugged. "Nobody's saying 'or else.' But it *is* getting hard on the rest of us. We've got to start thinking about things like the Miss Oak Grove contest, the spring play, and Senior Awards. None of us can afford to make many enemies."

The bell rang then, and everyone scattered. Bran walked with Keith to his next class...and although they held hands and Bran was perfectly attentive, Keith could tell that his mind was somewhere else.

*

Bran showed up at Keith's house about nine that night, after Mrs. Graff had unpacked and told Keith all about her trip. The older boy looked rather harried as Keith let him in and took his coat—Keith sat him at the kitchen table, put cookies and milk in front of him, and smiled. "What's up?"

"Kid...I've been doing a lot of thinking. Oh, God, you're going to think I'm copping out. Please don't get mad at me."

Keith took a breath. "I think I know what you're going to say."

"It's not just us. It's the whole gang. You understand that. I...well, we have to give some consideration to other people. Folks need time, and they need their own space. We won a battle—can't we relax for a bit and not push things too far too fast?"

"You think we shouldn't go to the dance."

"It's not personal, really it isn't. I love you, and I don't care who knows it. But like Jane said, maybe it would be better if we just...stayed in the background for a while." He smiled. "Valentine's Day, that'll be a whole different ball game."

What was he supposed to say?

"Bran, I do love you. After this weekend, I love you more than ever. You know I'll do anything for you. So if you think we should skip the dance," Keith forced a smile, "okay, we'll skip it."

Bran looked relieved. "I thought for sure you'd throw me out."

"Don't be silly. Like you say, there'll be other dances." Inside, Keith's stomach twisted in disappointment. But he couldn't let Bran know that. Bran was having a hard enough time as it was. Keith knew him well enough to know that when Bran said other people needed time and space, what he really meant was that *he* needed it.

"'Act well your part, there all the honor lies,'" Keith quoted. "If this is a part I have to act, then I'll act it well."

"And be covered with honor," Bran said, kissing him.

*

"I can't believe you did that."

"Give me a break, Frank."

It was Friday evening, the Friday of the Winter Dance. The last day of school was over, and Keith had called Frank to wish him a happy vacation and ask if he was going to visit over the holiday. When Frank asked how Bran was, Keith found himself blurting out the whole story.

"So you're staying home tonight. And what's Bran doing, going to the dance with his friends?"

"No. He's staying home too. Hey, fella, I thought you'd be delighted that I'm handling this in such an adult fashion."

"Adult, nothing. Keith, you're giving in to everyone else. So *what* if the whole school hates you?"

"Nobody hates me."

"Whatever. So what? You're going to let everyone else tell you what to do? You're going to let everyone else run your friendships?"

"We talked it over, Frank, and we decided it was best this way...."

"Damn it, Keith, stop being so grown-up for just one second." Frank paused, then said, "Do you want to go to the dance with him?"

"Yes. But —"

"But," Frank said with scorn. "But! Listen to me, Keith. I guarantee you that right this minute Bran is sitting at home wishing he could go to that dance with you. Instead, the two of you are going to cry yourselves to sleep in separate beds tonight."

"Suppose we went. What do we do about the rest of the school?"

"You stop caring about the rest of the school. You stop letting them run your lives." Frank's voice softened. "Fella, you love Bran and he loves you. The rest of the school has to learn to live with that, so they might as well start tonight. Knuckle under to them, and you'll hate yourself for the rest of your life."

Act well your part, Keith thought. There all the honor lies.

And what's my part? Bran said it—we are a team. Where I go, he goes.

I'm not acting that part very well, am I?

And where's the honor?

Keith was suddenly conscious of the clock. It was seven-thirty, and the dance started at eight.

"Frank...you're right. You've done it again. How can I thank you?"

He could almost see Frank's grin. "I'll think of some way. You might let me borrow Bran for a night...."

"Be serious."

"Don't worry about thanking me. Didn't you say that your dance starts in half an hour?"

"Yep."

"Then get on your way, brat. Call me tomorrow and let me know how things went."

"I will." Keith started to say goodbye, then stopped in mid-breath. "Frank?"

"Yeah?"

"I love you. More than I ever did."

"I know. And I love you. Now get on your way."

Keith pulled on his good pants and a shirt, fumbled in the bathroom mirror with his tie, and slipped into his suit jacket. After running a comb through his hair, he bounded downstairs and skidded into the kitchen where his mother was sewing.

"Mom, can I borrow the car and ten dollars?"

She chuckled. "Your tie's crooked. And you can't wear sneakers with that suit." She opened her purse, handed him two ten-dollar bills and the car keys. "Take twenty and bring me back the change. I take it you're going somewhere?"

Keith put the money and keys in his pocket, started unlacing his sneakers. "Yeah. Frank talked me into going to the dance."

"Alone?"

"No, I'm going to pick up Bran."

"I thought you fellows decided that discretion was the better part of valor?"

"I think I've changed my mind."

"Well, have a good time."

"I will." Keith ran upstairs, put on his good shoes, and then dashed out the door with a shouted "Goodbye!"

When he arrived at Bran's house he was relieved to see Bran's car in the driveway. It was just possible that his friend would have gone somewhere for the evening. At the front door, he took a deep breath, then knocked.

Bran's father opened the door. He raised his eyebrows. "Yes?"

"Hello, Mr. Davenport. I'm Keith Graff, a friend of Bran's. Is he in?"

"I'll go get him." Keith stood on the porch until Bran appeared and waved him in.

"What's this all about?" Bran said, gesturing to Keith's suit. "Are you selling something?"

"We're going to the dance," Keith said, breathless.

"I thought…."

"Come on, let's get you dressed."

Bran's room was smaller than Keith's, and cluttered with books, records, and a large stereo system. As he pulled clothes from his closet and changed, Bran said, "I thought we decided not to go to the dance."

"I thought so too. But the more I thought about it, the more I figured that it was time we stood up for ourselves."

"This is serious, Keith. Debbie's not going to like it—it might mean that she'll never talk to us again."

"It won't." Keith wasn't so sure what made him certain. "Remember the Thespian motto? Well, Bran, this is a part we've both got to act as well as we can. It's going to be our showdown with all the people who disapprove of us. And we've got to convince them that we're right."

"My, you're certainly ambitious tonight."

"I just got tired of being pushed around."

Bran shrugged into his jacket, then took a second to hug Keith. "This may be the biggest mistake we've ever made—but I'm sure glad you showed up. I was feeling really down in the dumps."

It was eight o'clock. "Let's go."

When they got to the school parking lot, Keith almost turned around and drove home. Then he forced himself to clam down. Whatever happens, he thought, this is something we've got to go through.

The cafeteria was decorated with green and silver garland and huge white cutout snowflakes; the band was loud but out in the hallway conversation was possible. Keith bought two tickets from a girl at the door, and then he and Bran walked in, hand in hand.

News of their arrival must have spread like a forest fire. Before they found the gang, Debbie found them. Everyone else tagged along behind her.

"I don't believe it," Debbie hissed. "Are you guys stupid, or what?"

"We've wised up, Debbie," Bran said.

"Bran Davenport, this is absolutely the last straw." Other students, sensing that they were missing out on something big, started crowding around. Keith felt as if he really were in a play—he had an audience, and he and Bran were on a stage of sorts.

If the other actors would only cooperate.

There was a subtle shift of position in the developing crowd. Laura and Bert stood next to Bran and Keith—Debbie and Warren faced them with the rest of the drama people on their side.

Tony Ramierez appeared with Susan Majors on his arm; he pushed past Laura and as he walked past he said to Bran, "Not a wise move, Davenport. I'm having trouble enough getting the Student Government to give us enough money for the Spring play—you may just have destroyed everything."

"And a Merry Christmas to you, too," Bran said. He took a step back. "Tony!" he called after Ramierez.

"What?"

"I want you to hear this, and I want Debbie to hear it too." Bran took a breath, straightened his back. Keith sensed that he was slipping into character. He didn't know, until much later, that the character was lawyer Clarence Darrow from *Inherit the Wind.*

"I love Keith, and some of you seem to think that I'm doing doing something really scandalous." Bran's voice, trained by his years of theater experience, boomed through the hallway. Nobody in earshot could help hearing him; nobody hearing him could help stopping to listen. "Okay, so Keith's new here, and he doesn't fit into the cliques. Who cares? I don't *do* cliques—I do acting, and I like to have friends around me who do the same thing I do.

"Keith's a junior, and I'm a senior," Bran continued. "And I'm sorry if you think that's wrong, but I happen to think that juniors are people too, and they deserve as much respect as everyone else."

There was a smattering of applause from the audience, and some movement of the crowd in Bran's direction.

"Tony, you're trying to hint that the Student Government is going to cut drama funds unless I get rid of Keith. That's the most stupid threat I've ever heard. We're drama people, and we don't accept blackmail from anyone. We're actors, we could put on a play in the middle of the football field if we wanted to. We could put on a play in the woods, the way they used to do in the middle ages. We could do Shakespeare without lights, without stage crew, and without royalties if we had to. Nobody tells us what we're going to perform, or how we're going to perform it." Keith could tell by the crowd's reaction that Bran had scored points with this announcement.

"There's one thing that's more important than everything else," Bran said, reaching for Keith's hand. "Jane, it concerns you and Rick...and Tony, it concerns you and Susan. And especially you and Warren, Debbie." He paused, holding everyone on the point of suspense, then said, "For everyone in this school who's in love, and everyone who's ever going to be in love...you know as well as I do that it's a fragile and wonderful thing. It can be broken by a lot of things...and one of them is pressure from other people. If you want to be free of that pressure, you have to learn to say 'No' to it. That's what

Keith and I are doing, and that's what the rest of you can do if you want."

Still holding Keith's hand, Bran pushed past the crowd. He started toward the cafeteria, where the band was playing on, oblivious of the drama being acted out in the hallway.

"Bran...wait." Debbie looked at the floor.

Bran turned to face her, raised an eyebrow.

Slowly, Debbie looked up at him. "I'm...I'm sorry for what I've done." A single tear glistened in her eyes, dropped to her cheek. "I love you, Bran, I always have and I always will. I n-never meant to hurt you. I never meant to drive you away. It just...just turned out that way."

Debbie took a step toward him, and Bran put an arm around her. She put her head on his shoulder and sobbed.

"Love doesn't have to be like that, Debbie," Bran said quietly. "Just because I love Keith doesn't mean I don't love you."

"I was so afraid that I'd lost you, and I just wanted to...to get rid of you before I got hurt more."

Laura put a comforting hand on Debbie's shoulder, and Keith covered it with his own. Debbie looked up at him, her eyes red and tears streaming down her cheeks now. "You must hate me. All the things I've said and done."

Keith surprised himself by leaning forward and kissing her on the cheek. "I never hated you, Debbie, and I can't now. We're all friends. Forever."

Bran spread his arms, embraced Keith on one side and Debbie on the other. Laura, Bert, Warren, Jane, and Rick folded into the circle.

Tony Ramierez stomped off in disgust, but the crowd stayed behind and applauded.

Bran laughed and joined hands with Keith and Debbie. In a second the whole gang was linked, and they bowed first one way, then the other, exactly as if they were performing a curtain call. Then, chuckling and hugging one another, they went to the dance floor where the band was just beginning to play a slow dance.

Pressed against Bran and surrounded by the others, Keith smiled in the darkness. We have each other, he thought. And we have our friends. Somehow, we've all survived. By being ourselves, not what others want us to be.

That's the greatest part we can all play.

And there all the honor *does* lie.

The Scattered Worlds Mosaic by Don Sakers

Dance for the Ivory Madonna
a romance of psiberspace
Print & Kindle
Spectrum Award finalist; 56 Hugo nominations
"Imagine a Stand on Zanzibar written by a left-wing Robert Heinlein, and infused with the most exciting possibilities of the new cyber-technology." -Melissa Scott, author of Dreaming Metal, The Jazz

Weaving the Web of Days
a tale of the Scattered Worlds
Print & Kindle
Maj Thovold has led the Galaxy for three decades, a Golden Age of peace and prosperity. She is weary and ready to resign, but she faces one last battle: a battle on the strangest battlefield known: a web of living tendrils that stretches across interstellar space. A web where Maj's enemies wait, like spiders, for their prey....

The Eighth Succession
a novel of the Scattered Worlds
Print & Kindle
"Remember when science fiction used to be filled with galactic intrigue and bigger-than-life heroes? The wonderful Don Sakers certainly does! The Eighth Succession is a rip-roaring yarn, impossible to put down. If John W. Campbell's Astounding Stories had been published in an LGBT-friendly era, this is the cover-story serial you'd have been waiting anxiously for each month. What a ride!" -Robert J. Sawyer, Hugo Award-winning author of Red Planet Blues

Children of the Eighth Day
a novel of the Scattered Worlds
Print & Kindle
The Eighth Succession *introduced readers to the Hoister Family...* Children of the Eighth Day *takes the story of this remarkable family to the exciting next level.*

The Scattered Worlds Mosaic by Don Sakers

All Roads Lead to Terra
two tales of the Scattered Worlds
Kindle only
Two exciting tales tell of attacks against the shining jewel of the Terran Empire: Earth. Includes an introduction and notes from the author.

A Voice in Every Wind
two tales of the Scattered Worlds
Print & Kindle
On a world where meaning lives in every rock and stream, and every breeze brings a new voice, one human explorer stands on the threshold of discoveries that could alter the future of Humanity.

A Rose From Old Terra
a novel of the Scattered Worlds
Print & Kindle
Jedrek left the Grand Library and his work circle eleven years ago. Now a crisis in uncharted space brings the circle back together. Soon, Jedrek and his friends are at the focal point of a clash of cultures, and the only thing that can save the Galaxy is one modest group of Librarians.

The Leaves of October
a novel of the Scattered Worlds
Print & Kindle
Compton Crook Award finalist
The Hlutr: Immensely old, terribly wise…and utterly alien. When mankind went out into the stars, he found the Hlutr waiting for him. Waiting to observe, to converse, to help. Waiting to judge…and, if necessary, to destroy.

More Books from Speed-of-C Productions

The Curse of the Zwilling by Don Sakers
Print & Kindle
*It's Hogwarts meets Buffy at Patapsco University: a small, cozy liberal arts
college like so many others – except for the Department of Comparative
Religion, where age-old spells are taught and magic is practiced. When a
favorite teacher is found dead under mysterious circumstances, grad student
David Galvin finds that a malevolent evil has awakened. And now David,
along with four novice undergrads, must defeat this ancient, malignant
terror.*

The SF Book of Days by Don Sakers
Print only
*Drawn from the pages of classic sf literature, here is a science fiction/fantasy
event for every day of the year...and for quite a few days that aren't part of
the year. From Doc Brown's arrival in Hill Valley (January 1, 1885) to the
launch of the* Bellerophon *(Sextor 7, 2351), this datebook is truly out of
this world.*

PsiScouts #1: At Risk by Phil Meade
Print & Kindle
*In the 26th century, psi-powered teenagers from all over the Myriad Worlds
join together as the heroic PsiScouts.*

Meat and Machine: queer writings by Don Sakers
Print & Kindle
*Don Sakers has been queering sf and fantasy for three decades. Meat and
Machine collects 24 short pieces of Don's science fiction, fantasy, nonfiction,
and erotics.*

Elevenses by Don Sakers
Print & Kindle
Eleven SF and fantasy short stories intended as bite-size snacks.

More Books from Speed-of-C Productions

Gaylaxicon Sampler 2006
Print only
Sample the work of thirteen writers from across the spectrum of gay, lesbian, bisexual, and/or transgender science fiction, fantasy, and/or horror. Includes big names and small, much-published veterans and promising beginners, Lammy and Spectrum Award nominees and winners, past Gaylaxicon Guests of Honor, and fresh new names.

QSpec Sampler 2007
Print only
Originally prepared as a giveaway at Gaylaxicon 2007 in Atlanta, this volume is available at a nominal charge as a sampler of the fine work being done by GLBT writers in SF, fantasy, and horror.

Lucky in Love by Don Sakers
Print & Kindle
When his best friend Keith moved away, there was a big hole left in Frank's life. Then a bad car crash put him in the hospital. While there recovering, he got a visit from the star of his high school basketball team, Purnell Johnson. It wasn't long before his luck started to improve.

Five Planes by Melissa Scott & Don Sakers
Print & Kindle
Space opera adventure. Pirates. Judges. Weird physics. Desperate refugees. Struggling colonists. Missing persons and a mystery ship. A quest for human origins in a pocket universe.

A Cosmos of Many Mansions: Varieties of SF by Don Sakers
Print & Kindle
Based on the first five years of Sakers's popular review column, this volume examines & explains dozens of types of science fiction along with hundreds of reviews.

The Mud of the Place by Susanna J. Sturgis
Print only
"A sensitive, witty, and tightly plotted portrayal of life on Martha's Vineyard that only a true Islander could have written. Nice going, Susanna!" –Cynthia Riggs

Printed in Great Britain
by Amazon

71295083R00108